"I'm Asking You To Marry Me, Ariel."

"Why?"

"What do you mean, why? Why does any man ask a woman to marry him?"

"We hardly know each other, Luke. Why are you putting me on the spot like this?" She stood abruptly, needing to get away from the ring Luke had taken out of the box and held now between his thumb and forefinger, as if he could just slide it right on her hand, branding her as his. "Tell me why, after six days, you've come to the decision that we could spend the rest of our lives together."

"We're sexually compatible, we like each other and I don't think you'd object to having a large family. I know all I need to know."

It was easier to argue with him than to dissect her feelings right then—and the fact that he wasn't mentioning love….

Dear Reader,

Where do you read Silhouette Desire? Sitting in your favorite chair? How about standing in line at the market or swinging in the sunporch hammock? Or do you hold out the entire day, waiting for all your distractions to dissolve around you, only to open a Desire novel once you're in a relaxing bath or resting against your softest pillow...? Wherever you indulge in Silhouette Desire, we know you do so with anticipation, and that's why we bring you the absolute best in romance fiction.

This month, look forward to talented Jennifer Greene's *A Baby in His In-Box*, where a sexy tutor gives March's MAN OF THE MONTH private lessons on sudden fatherhood. And in the second adorable tale of Elizabeth Bevarly's BLAME IT ON BOB series, *Beauty and the Brain*, a lady discovers she's still starry-eyed over her secret high school crush. Next, Susan Crosby takes readers on The Great Wife Search in *Bride Candidate #9*.

And don't miss a single kiss delivered by these delectable men: a roguish rancher in Amy J. Fetzer's *The Unlikely Bodyguard;* the strong, silent corporate hunk in the latest book in the RIGHT BRIDE, WRONG GROOM series, *Switched at the Altar*, by Metsy Hingle; and Eileen Wilks's mouthwatering honorable Texas hero in *Just a Little Bit Pregnant*.

So, no matter *where* you read, I know *what* you'll be reading—all six of March's irresistible Silhouette Desire love stories!

Regards,

Melissa Senate

Melissa Senate
Senior Editor
Silhouette Desire

SUSAN CROSBY

BRIDE CANDIDATE #9

SILHOUETTE Desire®
TM
Published by Silhouette Books
America's Publisher of Contemporary Romance

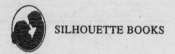

SILHOUETTE BOOKS

ISBN 0-373-76131-7

BRIDE CANDIDATE #9

This edition published by arrangement with Harlequin Books S.A.

Printed in U.S.A.

Books by Susan Crosby

Silhouette Desire

The Mating Game #888
Almost a Honeymoon #952
Baby Fever #1018
Wedding Fever #1061
Marriage on His Mind #1108
Bride Candidate #9 #1131

SUSAN CROSBY

is fascinated by the special and complex communication of courtship, and so she burrows in her office to dream up warm, strong heroes and good-hearted, self-reliant heroines to satisfy her own love of happy endings.

She and her husband have two grown sons and live in the central valley of California. She spent a mere 7½ years getting through college, and finally earned a B.A. in English a few years ago. She has worked as a synchronized swimming instructor, a personnel interviewer at a toy factory, and a trucking company manager. Involved for many years behind the scenes in a local community theater, she has made only one stage appearance—as the rear end of a camel! Variety, she says, makes for more interesting novels.

Readers are welcome to write to her at P.O. Box 1836, Lodi, CA 95241.

For Charlotte Brewer, an extraordinary bookseller
and a treasured friend, with love and thanks.
You've made such a difference in my life.

One

It was a short list, considering he was thirty-four years old, financially secure, reasonably good-looking and practically a household name. Luke Walker leaned back in his office chair and held a piece of paper aloft, contemplating the list he'd typed a few days ago while experimenting with his new computer. A nice, neat list of names. Eight potential candidates for the permanent job of Mrs. Lucas Walker.

Luke flipped the paper onto his desktop, then spun his chair to face the window behind him and the view of the mountains, frosted with fresh January snow, looking as stark and daunting as his life.

Too many changes at once. He acknowledged that. After a lifetime of knowing who and what he was, he no longer had a clue. But an offhanded question from a reporter recently had planted an idea—now was as good a time as any to settle down and start a family. After all, the more new roles he could assume, the quicker he could find out where he would settle for the rest of his life.

He heard his office door open and close.

"Luke, your two-o'clock appointment is here."

He searched his memory, drawing a blank, before he turned around. "I have an appointment?"

The assistant he'd inherited strode to his computer, punched a few keys and brought up his date book. "There. Two o'clock. Ariel Minx."

"Ariel Minx?" He leaned forward to look at the monitor himself. "Hell must've frozen over."

Silence hovered between them for a few seconds before his assistant spoke again. "I don't think I'll ask. She called early this morning and said she needed to see you, that it was urgent. You were in conference. Your message icon is lit, Luke." A long-suffering sigh was built into her words.

"I haven't mastered that function yet." A sudden, clear image of Ariel Minx came to mind—blond, delicate, average height. She'd filled out a basic black one-piece swimsuit to perfection. Nice shoulders, too, he recalled, and an elegant back—things he didn't usually notice on a woman.

"Is this business or pleasure with Miss Minx, Luke? Do you need me to take notes?"

His gaze drifted to the list of names, which he then shoved into his top drawer. "Business, I suspect. We met on that charity cruise last summer. Give me a minute, Marguerite, then show her in. If I need you, I'll let you know."

As soon as Marguerite left the room, Luke scooped up the crutches leaning against his desk and propelled himself across his office, swiping his suit jacket from a rack as he passed it. His crutches belonged in the bathroom, out of Ariel's sight and curiosity, on the off chance this wasn't a business call.

He had no intention of becoming another of her charitable causes.

Ariel Minx's instincts were usually good, but she hadn't pegged Lucas Walker at all. The office of the former star receiver of the San Francisco Gold Dusters and now president of Titan Athletic Shoes should have been gaudy with masculine pretense. It wasn't.

Ariel turned a slow circle as she waited for him to arrive. She'd anticipated a giant trophy room of gleaming tributes to his years as a professional football player. At the very least, his six *Sports Illustrated* covers, framed for public viewing and admiration, should have peppered his walls. Perhaps even a mounted animal head or two, in keeping with his all-American-male image.

She figured he fished and hunted with the best of 'em, given his penchant for tall tales. But, if so, such manly pursuits weren't in evidence here in his amazingly understated, tastefully decorated office, the furnishings of which were chosen for comfort, the arrangement cozy. She was drawn to the view of the Sierra Nevada mountains, and knew that beautiful Lake Tahoe was nestled a ridge away. She'd passed it on the way to Luke's office building.

Damn the man, anyway. She couldn't even fault him for having poor taste—and he'd been hard enough to resist with his more obvious liabilities.

"Well, Miz Minx, if you aren't a welcome sight for these sorry eyes." He filled the room with his presence as he came through a door, shutting it before he added, "What brings you out of the big city?"

In casual wear he had been imposing, she recalled. In a tuxedo, he'd all but sent her into a swoon. But then, most men looked good in a tux. Dressed for success, however, he overwhelmed. The navy blue fabric of his suit matched his eyes. A splash of burnished gold in his tie coordinated with his hair, gleaming brilliantly in the mid-afternoon sun shining through a picture window, freeze framing him in her mind.

"Cat got your tongue?" His eyes danced with friendly humor, as if he'd last seen her six days ago instead of six months.

Ariel frowned. He'd flustered her from the moment they'd met. She, who was always in control, chairing committees, not just serving on them. She, who managed a portfolio worth millions; she, who successfully sweet-talked celebrities and politicians into giving time and money to charitable causes, was reduced to struggling to find the right words with him.

Which was why she'd avoided him since the cruise she'd arranged and he'd attended as a sports celebrity—before his unexpected retirement. And if she'd been surprised or even a little disappointed that he'd taken her at her word and not contacted her during the ensuing months, she hadn't thought about it more than, oh, a couple of times a day.

She focused on the ever-present cigar that he grinned around. "Good afternoon, Mr. Walker. Still stinking up rooms, I see."

With a chuckle, he pulled the cigar from his mouth and ground it out in a nearby ashtray. He led her to a burgundy leather sofa, then sat beside her. He fingered the sleeve of her red wool suit. "Dressed like this, you must mean business."

He was a toucher. She'd forgotten that. He must be a wonderful lover— Ariel blinked, cannoning the image away, not for the first time. "I have a favor to ask," she said abruptly. "I thought it should be in person."

"Would you like something to drink?" He didn't wait for her answer, but pressed a button on a speaker phone. "Marguerite, would you get Miz Minx and me a fresh pot of tea, please?"

"I'd be glad to, Luke," came the immediate response.

"'It should be in person'?" he repeated to Ariel, not skipping a beat.

She shifted her gaze from the intercom to his face. "What if I'd wanted coffee?"

"You don't drink coffee."

"And how do you know that?"

"Why, Ariel, we shared quite a few meals on the cruise. You always ordered tea. Plain tea. No fancy flavors. No sweetener. No milk. A smart man pays attention to what a lady in his company prefers. Now, the woman who sat on my other side—''

''The one you were setting your sights on that first night, until her husband joined her?''

His eyes twinkled. ''I was just bein' friendly.''

''Uh-huh.''

''She liked margaritas—and keep 'em coming. And the lady across the table drank only milk. Six months pregnant, you recall.''

''Which leaves Mrs. Kent...''

''She enjoyed her sherry, didn't she?''

He waited, a challenge in his silence.

''Am I supposed to be flattered that you remember my tastes, Lucas, when you can also remember everyone else's?''

''Can't say the issue was whether you should be flattered, darlin'. Only that I noticed.''

Reluctantly Ariel smiled. Something else she'd forgotten—how easily he'd made her laugh. How much fun he was with his born-and-bred Texas drawl and understated humor. He'd been the only unmarried celebrity on the cruise, so at times—most of the time, actually—they'd ended up as a pair. He hadn't harassed her. He hadn't even looked at her with lust. But as soon as they'd become a couple by default, he'd monopolized her attention, entertaining her with stories that could as easily have been truth as fancy, and chipping away at the wall she'd built instantly between them, knowing she couldn't handle him in the way she handled any other man.

Before they returned to port, he'd managed to chip that wall low enough to step over. But when he'd asked to see her after the trip, she'd automatically said no—and he'd respected her wishes. She'd become more grateful as time passed, coming to believe it would have been just another shipboard romance.

But seeing him again made the feelings resurface fast enough to give her the bends.

Maybe she was making a huge mistake coming to him for help—

"What can I do for you, darlin'?" he asked in a tone so tender she almost threw her arms around him. Had her face revealed her feelings so vividly? She pushed her shoulders back and lifted her chin. "I'm here on business, Lucas. Strictly business."

"'Lucas,'" he repeated, angling her way. "No one but my grandmother calls me that. Same prickly tone of voice, too."

"I'm sorry," she said, then rested her shoulders against the cushions, making herself relax. "I'm under a lot of pressure right now. I don't mean to take it out on you."

"I'm just such an agreeable target."

"Too agreeable. You shouldn't let me get away with it so easily." She touched the back of his hand in apology.

He turned his hand over and entwined his fingers with hers. "You *have* abused my tender sensibilities upon occasion."

Ariel's breath caught. He'd held her hand on the cruise now and then, mostly in public, when he needed her to seem like his date in order to avoid a fawning fan. And he'd held her chair for her at meals, then touched her shoulder or arm briefly before moving on to take his own seat.

And they'd danced. He was an incredible dancer, but it wasn't his smooth moves that had triggered a shortness of breath or a rise in body temperature. There'd been something magical about the connection she felt with him, stronger than she'd ever felt for any man.

She might have accepted his invitation to see him after the cruise, too, if she hadn't been so afraid of the attraction. He was a man who graced magazine covers, a man who lived in the spotlight, a place she couldn't ever afford to be again, not if she wanted to keep what she'd worked so hard to achieve.

Regardless, they were too different in too many other ways. Compared to her slight frame, he was too big. A humble bone didn't live in his body. He didn't walk; he swaggered. He was forever chomping on that infernal cigar. His chest was hairy. He wasn't anything like any other man she'd dated. Not even close.

And yet...the mere touch of his fingers to hers reduced her to jelly. She looked from their joined hands to his face. He seemed content just to sit there with her, not saying anything, which was staggeringly out of character. He tended to talk a charmingly outrageous blue streak.

After a minute his assistant, a stunning brunette in her mid-twenties, came into the room, carrying a tray with a teapot, two mugs and a plate of cookies. Ariel tried to slide her hand from his.

"Will there be anything else?" Marguerite asked.

"No interruptions, please."

"Yes, sir."

After the door closed, Luke released her hand and picked up the teapot.

"You don't have to entertain me. I came here on business," Ariel said, noting how gracefully he poured even though his hands were large, his fingers long.

"Well, now, I don't know how you do business, but I kinda like to ease into it." He passed her a mug. "I've got plenty of time for you."

"I'll bet you don't hold hands with most of your associates."

He turned his head her way and flashed a smile. "You'd be right about that, darlin'."

"Or call them *darlin'*."

"Right again." He picked up his mug and almost took a sip. "Haven't seen any of them in swimsuits either. But that's neither here nor there," he continued. "So, I can see you're all tensed up. Why don't you tell me what's goin' on?"

Luke sipped his tea and watched her wrap both hands around her mug. She was nervous, he could see that. Why?

he wondered. Him or the reason that had brought her here? He couldn't wait to find out.

"Oh, it's this Couch Potatoes Mash event I cooked up. Your team getting into the Super Bowl has ruined it. And it looks like I've gotten all these kids' hopes up for nothing. Which happens far too frequently in their lives. And I really want this—"

"Hold on, there, Ariel." He stretched an arm along the cushion behind her. "Start at the top."

She blew out a breath. "I had this brilliant idea to have a mid-winter, let's-get-our-butts-off-the-couch event to raise funds for the Wilson Buckley Youth Center in San Francisco. Have you heard of it?"

"Can't say as I have."

"It's an excellent facility, with the highest standards and a tremendous staff in a pretty tough neighborhood of the city. My vision was a whole day of competition for the kids, kind of a mini-Olympics, followed by a dinner-dance and silent auction for adults. I figured I could get local businesses to sponsor individual athletic events. The publicity would draw more kids into the center and show them there are safe places they can go and have fun, particularly during the middle of winter. We planned it for the last weekend in January."

"Super Bowl weekend," he said, looking away from her.

"Which is less than two weeks from now, as you know. Well, no one expected the Gold Dusters to make the Super Bowl without— Well, without *you.* All the sports writers said so, and for most of the season, it looked like they'd be right. Then, you know what happened."

He took a controlled sip of his tea, needing a moment before he responded. "They came to life."

"Did they ever! But now I'm in a big jam, Lucas, and I hope you can help me out of it."

"Go on."

"The Center is privately funded. They get no government support of any kind. They've just completed a major remodeling so that they can handle a fifty-percent increase in membership. Financially, they're in deep, though. Several of the Gold Dusters had promised to support the event, but now that they're in the Super Bowl, they can't. The game's the next day. Without them, interest is lagging."

He stood and wandered to the window, keeping his back to her. He was glad to see her but— "Why don't you just change the date?"

"We could, but everything's in place. It was a lot to set up. I even got some of the kids involved, Lucas. They took part in the meetings with the local business owners so they could see how the system works—how to negotiate, how to deal with people different from themselves. They've got a lot at stake here, not the least of which is their need for people to believe in them and their genuine needs. If I can't drum up a major sponsor for the event, we'll lose everything we've put into it. At this point, we'd settle for breaking even and doing something again in the summer."

"Which leads you to why you've come, I suppose. You want my company to take over sponsorship."

"Would you? It would mean so much to the kids."

He let the words sink in as he turned around. He couldn't let his pride get in the way of an important cause. The look of expectation on her face made his stomach clench. He cocked his head. "You haven't done this before, have you, darlin'?"

"Done what?"

"Fund-raising."

Ariel fidgeted. "What makes you say that?"

"'Cause you're goin' about it all wrong." He carried his mug with him to his desk. "You're supposed to approach your target expecting positive results. You should be anticipating my objections. You should be sayin' things to let me try on the idea of involving myself. Now, I'm not sayin' that usin' the emotional approach won't work, but a seasoned fund-raiser saves that tactic for last."

"You're limping."

"Nice change of subject. Smooth, Ariel. Real smooth." He chuckled and shook his head.

"Well, you *were*. I thought you'd had surgery. Didn't it work?"

"It worked. Rehab takes longer than you might think. It's no big deal." He booted his computer and typed a few words.

"I was sorry to hear about your having to retire," she said. "That must be really hard on you."

"Not as hard for me as others, maybe. I had the company to turn to. I've worked for Titan since I was twenty-two, off and on. My grandfather decided it was a good time for him and my grandmother to see America, so it worked out all the way around."

Ariel wondered if he was deluding himself that he could give up that part of his life so easily, or if he was trying to delude her. Men. Such tough guys. Can't ever let anyone see them vulnerable.

She couldn't sit still as he spent the next few minutes at his computer, looking at his budget—she hoped—for what he could swing for a donation.

She strolled to the window behind him. She ran a mental list of the advice that the foundation's professional fund-raiser had given her, deciding she'd messed things up because she hadn't factored in her own emotional response to seeing him again. Ariel had decided to meet personally with Luke, alone without the fund-raiser, since she had the advantage not only of having met him but of having spent a lot of time with him.

But Luke was right. She wasn't any good at asking people for help. Which was why she usually just dove in and did things herself instead of begging someone else. She glanced at the back of his head, wondering if she should tell him how desperate she was for his help.

"Any chance you missed me some?" he asked out of the blue, then turned and leveled a penetrating stare on her.

She cupped her mug a little tighter. "A slight chance."

"Slight, as in 'a passin' thought once a week'? Or slight, as in 'way too much but I won't let him know that'?"

"Somewhere in between."

He tapped a pencil on his desk. "Are you ever gonna cut me any slack? I didn't do anything but admire you."

"You monopolized my time so I couldn't spend it with anyone else. I had lots of friends aboard the cruise. Friends who are more like family. I didn't get to spend time with them thanks to you."

"Family," he repeated thoughtfully, tipping his chair back. "Now, there's a word to consider. What defines a family to you?"

She frowned. "People you care about, of course. People you love. People you can count on."

"So, they don't have to be related by blood?"

"If that were the case, I'd have a family of one." She regretted the words the minute she said them, because his gaze softened pitifully.

"Who would that be?"

"My Aunt Bonnie, the wildest, craziest woman you could ever hope to meet."

"In what way?"

"In every way. She didn't believe in staying put for longer than a few months, so I grew up traveling around Europe. It was quite an education." She set her mug on his desk. "What's your answer, Lucas? Will you help or will those poor kids be at the mercy of the streets? Their futures lie in your hands."

"Oh, that's good, Ariel. It'd be my fault if they turned into delinquents, right?"

"You could make a difference."

A computerized female voice announced that e-mail awaited his attention. He punched a couple of keys, read the words that came up on the screen, shut it down, then moved to stand beside Ariel.

"Why did you come to me for help?" he asked.

"You seem to march to your own drummer. I thought if

anyone could pull this off at the last minute, you could. I know that companies usually decide what and how they're going to donate early in their fiscal year, but I was hoping you'd override your board of directors and pitch in. I also figured you'd be in town, anyway, for the game, so you might be able to drop in personally."

"Well…you figured wrong."

Two

"I see." Ariel stiffened. She felt as if she'd just gained a hundred pounds, most of it in her feet, which she was afraid weren't going to move forward on command and get her out of here before she made a bigger fool of herself. "I'm sorry to have taken up so much of your time. I can see myself out."

"I haven't said no. When I said you figured wrong, I meant about my coming into the city for the Super Bowl. The rest might be manageable."

Her uncooperative feet stayed rooted. She smoothed her suit jacket down her stomach, fidgeted with the brass buttons, fussed with her purse strap. She'd counted on him—maybe for more than just his help out of a jam.

"I've just requested information from the comptroller regardin' how much we could do for you, financially and with product," he said. "He'll bring the answers when he has them. But I'll also need to check out the Center before we commit. We have to choose our causes carefully. Public opinion is what drives this company. And a good product, of course. We're on our way up. We can't afford to become involved in anything remotely questionable."

Ah. So here was the hard-hearted businessman she hadn't met. Good. He wasn't merely a figurehead. She didn't know why that pleased her so much, but it did. His image— Well, she'd been wrong about him. That's all that mattered. "I'm sure you'll be pleased with what you find, Lucas. But money alone can't save this event from total devastation. It's going to take a public show of commitment to the cause. From Titan *and* you. You're the key."

"Is your reputation on the line, too?"

"That's the least of it."

"Is it? Titan has credibility, enough credibility to turn things around. I need to know something, Ariel. Did you exhaust every other possibility? Was I your last resort?"

She shook her head. "You were the first person I thought of. The first person I turned to. The truth is, I'm desperate. We can't afford the loss of publicity at this point. You're high profile in San Francisco. You could make the difference."

He looked away from her for a moment, then shifted his weight slightly.

"If I determine there's no reason not to," he said, "I'll add the weight of Titan's name to your cause. Now, don't get that all-hopeful look yet. There are hurdles to jump first."

"For me or for you?" Her heart did a little dance at his softening expression.

"Maybe both." He brushed his fingers along her hair, a feather-light touch. "You know, I hadn't seen you with your hair up. I kinda miss the way all that honey blond silk flows around your shoulders and down your back. I can't remember those big brown eyes of yours bein' so dark and mysterious either. Tell me you missed me, darlin'."

"Like a fly misses a swatter, *darlin'*."

He moved a little closer. "I wanted to kiss you that last night on the cruise. You kinda ruined the mood when I asked to see you again and you told me sure, as soon as hell froze over.''

''So you remembered. I was hoping you wouldn't.''

He ran a finger along her jaw. ''I doubt I forgot much about you.''

She listened to her heart pound. ''Not too many women turn you down, I imagine.''

''Just 'cause I'm kinda well-known, doesn't mean I'm not out there scroungin' for dates on Friday night like every other man. I've had my share of turn-downs.''

''I find that a little hard to believe. One of the magazine articles I read about you called you a party animal, or something like that.''

He toyed with her earring, just barely brushing the skin below it with his thumb. ''Amazin' what a well-paid personal publicist, not to mention a team publicist can do for a man's image, isn't it? I might've kicked up my heels now and then, but I wasn't nearly as busy as the media liked to paint me. Women weren't beatin' down a path to my door, darlin'. Sure made for good press, though.''

Even though her skin rose in bumps of reaction to his touch, she held herself perfectly still. ''Maybe you need to give up those cigars you're so fond of. Personally, I've never understood how any woman kisses a man who smokes cigars.''

''Well, now, that part's simple, Ariel.'' He framed her face with both hands and lowered his head. ''Like this.''

Any thought of resistance evaporated in a heartbeat, perhaps because she'd been waiting for this moment. Hoping for it. At the touch of his lips, she took flight in a long, slow takeoff of reaction, soared in a current that kept her adrift and astonished and mesmerized. At the feel of his arms enfolding her, she began a free fall of delight and desire and something close to fear. He wasn't supposed to taste this good, or feel so familiar, or fill so many needs at once. His smoky scent only added to his appeal, making him so distinctive, so much his own man. So much a man she wanted.

When he lifted his head, she was overwhelmed with the need to stay in his arms and be held. He let her go too soon.

Here was the biggest risk. Not the Center, no matter how important that was, but her heart, which was in much greater danger of being lost. She'd known that from the moment she'd met him. Known it and ignored it. Known it and denied it. She still had to make sure she didn't fall under his spell. He was far too public a person.

Someone knocked on the door. At Luke's invitation, a man walked in, a very tall man with the distinctive look of a Walker about him.

"I've got that information for you, Luke."

"Sam, I'd like you to meet Ariel Minx. You're gonna be spending a little time gathering some data from her. Ariel, this is my cousin, Sam Walker. He's Titan's comptroller."

"I noticed the resemblance," she said, shaking off the kiss, trying to settle her feet back on the ground and pull her head from the clouds. "I figured you were brothers, though."

"Close as," Sam said. He looked at Luke. "Are we working here or in my office?"

"Here. Three heads will be better than two, in this instance." He slid his jacket off and loosened his tie. "Grab yourself a cup of coffee, Sam. We'll be here awhile."

From his office window, Luke watched Ariel climb into her Explorer. Snow wasn't predicted for tonight, but he was glad she had four-wheel drive, just in case. The thought of her driving to San Francisco at night, a three- to four-hour trip, depending on traffic, bothered the hell out of him. He hadn't been able to convince her to stay over, though. Too many obligations at home, she'd said. Obligations. Her middle name, apparently. She worked more than full-time, and all as a volunteer.

"Drop your pants, Luke."

Ignoring the distinctly feminine command, Luke waited until Ariel's car was out of sight before kicking off his shoes and unbuckling his belt. The running shorts he wore underneath were a new style and would hit the retail market next month. He'd expected to wear them himself. In training, that is. It wasn't going to happen now. Hell, he'd be lucky to walk without a hitch for the rest of his life—provided his surgery went well.

"Hurry up. My hands are freezing," Marguerite complained.

He limped to the sofa, took the towel she offered, then sucked in a fierce breath as she molded a plastic bag filled with ice over his knee. It had taken everything he'd had in him not to show Ariel how much he hurt.

"Do you want a pain pill?" Marguerite asked as he situated himself more comfortably.

"Just took one." He hated taking them, so he avoided it until the pain became unbearable. He shifted until he lay flat, shoving some pillows under his leg to elevate it above his heart.

"Exactly what was so all-fired important about this meeting that you couldn't use your crutches?"

"None of your business." His amiable tone dulled the impact of the words.

"Oh, I see. *This* is the one. Gotta be caveman for the potential wife." She snorted. "Her name wasn't on your list, the last I looked."

He opened one eye. "I don't recall seein' anything about badgerin' the boss in your job description."

"And I haven't seen anything about playing nurse, either, but I'm doing it. Quit being a baby."

Luke opened his other eye. "Lord, I feel sorry for Sam. I think I'd better clue him in about you before he's shackled for life."

"Sam knows what he's getting. He loves me *because* I'm bossy."

"And because you've got a body that won't quit," Sam said, appearing out of nowhere. He slid an arm around her waist.

"Won't quit what?" Marguerite teased him.

"Come with me, little girl, and I'll show you."

"Stop growling like some lecherous wolf, Sam, and take it somewhere private," Luke muttered.

"Jealous?"

"Hand me a cigar, then go home. Both of you."

Sam plucked a cigar from the humidor on Luke's desk, snipped off the end and passed it to his cousin, along with a lighter. "Are you all right?"

"Yeah." Luke caught the look that passed between Sam and Marguerite. "I'm fine. Don't worry about me. Turn off most of the lights, too, please."

He waited until the door closed before he groaned. As soon as the swelling subsided and the medication kicked in, he'd be able to function again. He knew the drill. Until then, he had to lie still.

He blew a smoke ring, then another. Sam's innocent query gave him pause. "Jealous?" he'd asked. Yeah, he was jealous. Jealous of Sam's unbroken body. Jealous of his having a companion to share his life with. But not jealous of his impending marriage, not when Luke could see how hot Sam was for Marguerite.

Luke had made that mistake twice in his life—confused lust for love. Not this time. This time he would choose a woman he knew would be a good companion outside of the bedroom. And someone who didn't want his money, either. He'd prefer a woman whose body was the exact opposite of either of his voluptuous ex-fiancées, a woman who didn't make him fantasize.

He knew what he wanted. Home and hearth. Continuity. They had to be on the woman's wish list, too.

He relaxed as his pain eased. Maturity hadn't sneaked up on him—it'd slapped him full in the face. First, with the arrival of his thirty-fourth birthday six months ago. Then the damned injury two months later. He might have tried to continue playing ball for another couple of years, hoping that he wouldn't totally destroy both knees, but he'd decided to stop sacrificing his body for his sport, difficult as that decision was.

Finally, the last big change, the sudden opportunity to take Titan to a whole new level of competition in the industry when his grandfather had turned over the presidency of the company to him. His entire life was going to be different from here on. A normal existence, finally. One where he wasn't taking orders from coaches and trainers and owners, but leading the team, instead, and deciding the future. And marriage, of course.

Lust wasn't going to make his decisions for him this time. Not that dubious emotion love, either, whatever that was. Nope. This time he was choosing a helpmate, a companion, a friend.

Gingerly, he swung his legs around and sat up. He'd already had surgery on one knee. Day after tomorrow, the other. Cautiously he stood, not moving until he got his balance, then he walked to his desk, switched on a light and opened his top drawer. He plucked a small velvet box from the corner he'd shoved it into and pushed up the lid. A flawless, three-carat diamond ring sparkled back at him. A ring his jeweler insisted any woman would be thrilled to wear. He snapped the lid shut and picked up his neatly typed list, examining it, top to bottom.

Each name was followed by the details he thought important. They represented a spectrum of professions—Realtor, two lawyers, orthopedic surgeon, physical therapist, actress, loan officer and television sportscaster. Five of them already had children—a definite advantage in his book—but it also meant an ex-husband to deal with forever because of kids being involved. Of the three childless women, he could conjure up the image of only one, the sportscaster for a San Francisco station, whom he'd met last year. He supposed he remembered her face because he'd seen her on television since.

Names. They were just names.

His plan suddenly seemed idiotic. Juvenile. And yet, how

else could he get what he wanted? He had to start somewhere.

He let the paper drift back onto the desk, the sound as it landed seeming to whisper a word. He glanced out his window at the darkening sky. A moment later he picked up a pencil and scrawled an addition to the list—the name that had been in his head trying to get out all afternoon:

9. Ariel Minx—

He hesitated. What did she do for a living? Did she have any children? He realized how little he knew about her.

Finally, he added: professional do-gooder. That made him smile.

He took the paper with him as he returned to the couch and stretched out again. He drew on his cigar, contemplating Ariel. He admired that she hadn't asked for help for selfish reasons. Had she begged his assistance for herself alone, he might have agreed without learning whether it made sense for Titan. She hadn't used that leverage.

Because she'd been so adamant about his not contacting her after the cruise, he hadn't considered her before, but he could see that she would make a good wife. A great hostess. A phenomenal mother. She wouldn't care that they'd have to adopt, either. She'd love those kids just the same as if she'd given birth to them.

The scent of her perfume drifted over him before he realized how impossible that was. He'd already filled the air with cigar smoke. Wait. There it was again. Soft and flowery. He turned his head toward the back of the couch and sniffed. The leather seemed to breathe her fragrance.

He smiled. That all-business suit and hairstyle had thrown him at first, not looking like his recollection of her. But the fire in her eyes hadn't changed. That she'd rebuffed him once before didn't matter. He had a clean slate, he figured, since she'd come to him.

He tried to recall their kiss, but he'd been in so much pain, he hadn't really been able to concentrate on it at the time. Without being able to put much weight on one leg, it was all he could do to stay upright. Still, if the lust had been strong enough, it would've wrestled the pain out of his mind, wouldn't it? Yeah. He was sure of that. He'd had plenty of experience with lust. He'd only kissed Ariel because she'd all but challenged him to.

Yeah, right. Got some other fairy tale on your mind, Luke?

He stared at her name before folding the paper carefully and sliding it into his shirt pocket. He could make his own rules this time—and there was no rule saying he had to start his search at the top of the list.

Three

Ariel hung up the phone and flopped back on her bed, covering her eyes with her arm. What a stubborn man Lucas Walker was. He hadn't succumbed to any carrot she'd dangled in front of him. Yes, Titan was going to save the Couch Potatoes event, but, no, Luke wouldn't make a personal appearance. She'd thought for sure she'd be able to convince him. Ha!

A week had flown past, with phone calls back and forth, faxes sent and received. In the end, Titan would not only be the largest sponsor of the event but would also provide each participant with a new pair of athletic shoes, as well as T-shirts not available to the public yet. Luke had lined up a ton of autographed sports paraphernalia, not just from football players, but from most other pro sports as well. The ticket sales for the dinner-dance and silent auction were twice what her committee had anticipated during the initial planning, three times what they were a mere week ago.

Sold out. She couldn't ask for more.

She was asking, however. She wanted him there, in person.

The thought curled around her like a drift of his cigar smoke, stinging her eyes. As long as she was being so honest with herself, she might as well take the truth the whole way—she wanted to dance with him again, to be in his arms again, maybe even kiss him again.

A memory of their last evening on the cruise had surfaced during the past week. She'd gone for a swim, enjoying the empty pool as everyone else partied. When she'd finally emerged, Luke had materialized out of the shadows, wrapping a towel around her from behind, his arms enfolding her, drawing her against him. Even through the fabric she'd felt the warmth of his body all the way down to her toes.

They'd stayed like that a minute or two, awareness sizzling. It was then that he'd asked to see her again.

She'd almost said yes. The truth was, she'd almost invited him to her cabin. Then someone walked by, calling his name, and she'd remembered his place in the world. Remembered the stack of *Sports Illustrated* magazines with him as the Super Bowl MVP on the cover that he'd autographed for the fans who'd donated big money just to be on the same cruise ship with him.

She'd found the strength to turn him down because of it. He didn't have a clue about how hard it had been for her to give up the chance to see him again, when, in fact, she'd found him charming, appealing, exciting and very, very tempting.

Luke seemed to have all the determination this time around, however. He had no intention of being in San Francisco while his team played in the Super Bowl. The pain of not playing was more than he could bear.

Oh, he hadn't said so, but she knew it.

The phone rang. She shoved herself up to answer it.

"Hi. It's me again. I know you're probably ticked off at me."

"I won't ask you again, Lucas. I promise. You're not coming. I accept it."

"Actually, I changed my mind."

"You did?"

"Under one condition. If I do your event, you do mine."

"I don't understand."

"I can't seem to get the Dusters' owner to take no for an answer. Everyone expects me in the box for the game. I'm asking you to go with me."

Ariel clutched the receiver closer. He didn't know what he was asking of her, of course. Didn't know that she shunned the spotlight—and why. Could she risk a public appearance with him?

Sacrifice. The word bound them together. They would both be sacrificing something. Hers was greater—

"Ariel? You there?"

"I'm here." She swallowed. "And you've got yourself a deal. Where will you stay, though? I heard on the news that every hotel is booked."

"Darlin', darlin'. You don't really think I'd have any trouble linin' up a room, do you? Celebrity has its perks."

The teasing tone didn't completely cover some emotion she couldn't quite name, but that she could hear, beneath the surface of the words. If he stayed in a hotel, he'd be hounded by the media. How many times could he answer the question of how it felt not being able to be part of history? She knew how intrusive the media could be.

She sighed at the inevitability of what she was destined to ask him next. First, sacrifice, now risk. "If you don't mind not having room service or the media camped outside your door, Lucas, why don't you just stay with me at my apartment?"

Unearthly silence followed. She filled it. "It'd sure make it easier all the way around. We've got to get to and from the Center, then the dinner-dance, and then the game. I think we know each other well enough to coexist for a few days. You have to leave the cigars at home, though."

"I wouldn't smoke in your house. Any other rules I should know of?"

"I don't know if you would consider it a rule, but, just so that there's no confusion, you will have a bedroom of your own. And this is a strictly platonic invitation."

"Naturally."

She swore she could hear him grinning. He had agreed to the stipulation way too fast.

"Okay, Ariel. I'll be there. Thanks for the offer."

"When will you arrive?"

"Wednesday night. I'd like to check everything at the Center ahead of time myself. I'm kinda curious, though, why you're makin' rules before they become issues. If you're afraid of something, why don't you just tell me now, and we'll settle it before we see each other."

"I'm not afraid of anything."

"Doesn't sound like it to me, Ariel."

When they ended the conversation a few minutes later, she wondered the same thing. The answer was easy. She was afraid of him and his very public life. She was also drawn to the vulnerable side of him, the tough guy who she decided didn't want the world to know how hard it was to leave his celebrity status behind, the identity of "football player," a role he'd had since he was a boy.

But something stronger had pushed and shoved its way past all that. The acknowledgment that she needed him, too. Needed to feel like a woman, cherished and valued for who she was, not because she was a quintessential volunteer and the ultimate hostess.

She just wanted the fantasy for a little while.

"This is stupid," Marguerite shouted as she ducked her head against the driving wind and rain bombarding San Francisco. "Just tell her the truth, Luke."

He returned a quelling look, then climbed the next stair. And the next.

"If she's any kind of woman, she won't care about your disability."

"I don't want to be coddled. And I'm not disabled permanently. I just decided to put off the surgery until after this weekend. Keep your voice down now. We're almost to the top. She'll hear us."

"Men," Marguerite muttered, hefting a rain-splattered bag.

"Including me in that tone of voice, sweetheart?" Sam asked, adjusting Luke's Pullman and suit bag as they ascended the stairs to Ariel's second-floor apartment.

"For the moment. Talk to him, Sam."

"It's like talking to granite, and you know it. He's—"

"Shh." Luke came to a stop at the landing. He resisted rubbing his aching knee. "Just set the bags down and scoot on back to the rental car. I'll take it from he—"

The door opened, spilling light on the three, who probably looked like five-year-olds caught playing doctor, Luke decided.

"Brought your entourage, Lucas?" Ariel asked, opening the door wider. "A big, strong man like you can't carry his own luggage?"

"Hello to you, too, darlin'." Lord, she looked good. He brushed past her, letting Sam and Marguerite follow. He got an impression of space and color and warmth as he glanced around her living room.

Ariel tossed a towel at Marguerite, then disappeared into a room and returned with a couple more for the men.

"Take off your jackets. I'll fix something to warm you up."

"They're not staying," Luke said.

"Don't be rude." Ariel gave him a direct look.

"I spend fifty to sixty hours a week with Luke as it is," Marguerite said. "You think I'd willingly subject myself to more?"

Sam chuckled. "Gotta get to the hotel." He passed the towel back to Ariel and placed a hand at Marguerite's back.

Ariel's brows lifted. "You have something urgent to do at ten-fifteen at night?"

"After the flight we just had, a hot bath and a stiff drink seem not only urgent, but a matter of life or death," Marguerite said.

"You flew here? I assumed you were so late arriving because the snowstorm in the Sierras made the roads tricky to drive."

"Blizzard," Luke corrected her, curious at her sudden pallor. "We sat on the tarmac for a couple of hours waiting for a window of opportunity."

"They should have canceled the flight."

"Once the tower granted permission, it was my call, since I'm the pilot," he said, then grabbed her arm when she swayed. "What's wrong with you?"

"You're a pilot? You flew *yourself* here?" she asked, her eyes huge and dark. "In a *blizzard?*"

"It was clear when we took off. Ariel, I've been flyin' for more than ten years. During the off-season I represented Titan all around the country. Flying myself saves a lot of time and hassle getting from place to place, but it's also my recreation. You have a problem with that?"

She shrugged, the color returning to her cheeks as she pulled free of his hold. "Nope."

"Good."

Marguerite snorted.

"Come on, sweetheart. We should get going," Sam said, tugging on her arm.

"Ariel," Marguerite called over her shoulder as she was being physically removed from the house, "make sure he doesn't climb your stairs too many times a day."

Luke took three long strides to reach the front door. He leaned around the jamb. "You're fired."

"Fine," she yelled back. "You're a pain in the butt to work for, anyway."

He grinned as he shut the door.

"That's funny?" Ariel asked.

"She either quits or I fire her once a week."

"But she doesn't leave, and you don't replace her, right?"

"She's engaged to my cousin. Where should I put my gear?"

Ariel blinked at the quick change of subject. She picked up the suit bag and led the way to the guest room. "What did Marguerite mean about not climbing my stairs?"

"Nothin' for you to worry about. My knee's been a little tender, that's all. I'm tryin' to rest it. Hadn't counted on your being up a flight."

She glanced at his legs, but didn't see anything unusual. No sign of a knee brace, no excess bulk from being wrapped. His jeans fit him from hips to ankles nicely. Very nicely, indeed.

He filled up the room, Ariel thought as she hung his bag in the closet. An average-size room to start with, it suddenly seemed tiny now, the queen-size bed too small for his frame, the quilt too dainty, the curtains too frilly. It wasn't that he was so big, actually. Although in comparison to herself, he was. He was just so…so much a man. One who was a little overbearing—well, maybe more than a little. And extremely appealing.

"Are you hungry?" she asked into the quiet that had settled between them. She didn't want to feel so comfortable with him.

"If you'd share a pot of tea with me, I'd be obliged."

"I never figured you for a tea drinker, Lucas. Coffee, black. Whiskey, straight. Steak, rare. That's what I would have expected."

"You got the rest of it right. Don't care much for coffee, though. Why don't I unpack, then I'll join you."

"Okay."

"Oh, Ariel?"

She turned in the doorway.

"This is a real nice place you've got here."

"Thanks. The view was the deciding factor for me. On a

clear day, you can see the world from my front window. Well, at least a good portion of San Francisco Bay."

Ten minutes later, he wandered into her kitchen and leaned against a counter. He'd exchanged his rain-soaked clothes for sweatpants, a T-shirt and socks. "I take it you were worried when I didn't show on time," he said.

"A little bit."

"It does my heart good to hear that, Ariel. Real good."

She poured a mug for each of them, not meeting his gaze. "I was afraid I'd have to find someone to take over all the jobs I've volunteered you to do."

He chuckled. "Afraid you might spoil me if you ever let a compliment cross your lips?"

"Too late for that. You were ruined long before I met you." They moved into the living room and sat on the sofa, one at each end. "I am in your debt, however, for what you've done for the Center."

"I'm glad I could help." Luke tried to get a handle on her mood. Except for her opening salvo when he'd first arrived, her insults weren't being delivered with much punch, as if she felt the need to get them out, but not engage in any bantering with him. "What's got you quiet as a cloud? Thinkin' up some new insult?"

She smiled slightly. "Actually, the quiet part you *should* take as a compliment. I'm tired. I generally hide that from most people."

She did look tired, now that he looked more closely. "Anything I can do?"

"I'll put you to work tomorrow. Sam and Marguerite, too, I guess. I'm assuming they're here to help."

"I promised the board of directors at the Center that we'd oversee the finances of this event. I want to make sure there's a profit, not just the break-even goal you said would satisfy you."

"No one told me that."

"Are you on the board?"

"No. I'm an angel, though. And this event was my idea."

"Well, now, I'd say your golden hair might lead some people to think you're wearin' a halo, but I'll bet Saint Peter's gonna give you grief at the Pearly Gates. He'll have seen the way you treat me."

She wrinkled her nose at him. "Benefactors are called angels. I'm on the board of the Angel Foundation, which contributes regularly to the Center."

"I'm curious about that, Ariel. How do you support yourself? As far as I've been able to determine, you're not employed."

"Interest." She tucked her feet under her and cupped the mug more closely.

"Interest?"

"On investments. People don't volunteer time the way they used to. I can afford to."

"You've got an MBA from Stanford, but you don't put it to work. Why's that?"

"Who says I don't put it to work?" She lifted the mug again, then lowered it to her lap. "How'd you know that, anyway?"

"Part of my investigation into the Center. I checked out everyone. We had so little time, we hired a PI." He tapped his fingers against his mug. "Funny thing. He didn't find any record of you before you enrolled at Stanford."

She took a quick sip of tea. "Why would that matter?"

"Professionally? For no reason. But personally? I was curious."

"What'd you expect to find?"

"Perfect attendance in elementary school? A driver's license issued on your sixteenth birthday? I don't know. A past. Apart from learnin' you're twenty-seven years old, you're Stanford educated, you've lived at this address for three years, and you donate your time to a lot of worthy causes, I don't know anything about you."

"There's nothing mysterious about it. I told you I grew up in Europe."

He noted that wariness had combined with weariness to

darken her eyes. "And you said you were tired. Me, too. Let's go to bed, darlin'." He took her empty mug and stood. "Now, don't you go lookin' at me like that. I wasn't bein' suggestive. I have nothin' but the utmost respect for you. I can't help it if you've got a dirty mind."

He returned from the kitchen just as she levered herself up from the couch. She shook her head.

"You're incorrigible, Lucas."

"Well, see, that's where you're wrong. I'm putty in your hands, just waitin' to be molded. So, what time do we get started in the morning?"

They walked across the living room. "I have to be at the senior citizens center at eight. You probably have friends or teammates you want to see, so feel free to do whatever you want until ten, then we should get over to the youth center."

"I don't think my hangin' around with the Dusters is a good idea. I'll tag along with you, instead."

"You'll probably be pretty bored."

"I doubt that." He pushed her hair back from her face; his fingertips grazed her temple.

Oh, hell. She was begging to be kissed. He could see it in the dark pull of her eyes and the way her lips parted. He stopped a sigh from escaping by pressing his lips to her forehead. "Sleep tight, darlin'."

She laid her hands flat against his chest and leaned into him. He didn't seem to have a choice other than to wrap his arms around her. He heard her sigh. He felt her nestle, her cheek rubbing his shoulder. Damned if she didn't feel good there, all cuddly and subdued. Wifely.

A moment later she pushed herself away. "I'm glad you made it here safely," she said, her words bright and cheery again. "Good night."

Intrigued by her changing mood, he half smiled and rubbed his jaw as she shut her door. "Good night?" He wondered.

Ariel dragged a towel along her throat, across her chest, down one arm, then the other. Her sweat-dampened pajama top lay discarded on the bed beside her. Her gaze flickered to the clock. Two-thirty. Her hand shook as she lifted the glass of water from her nightstand and gulped it down, not coming up for air until the glass was drained. She gasped a breath, managed to set down the glass, then blotted her face with the towel.

She wondered if she'd screamed. Probably not or Luke would have rushed in. She lay back and stared at the ceiling. Her skin tightened into a mass of goose bumps from nightmare sweat and winter cold.

She hadn't had the dream in so long. So very long.

And she knew exactly what had triggered its return.

She raised herself on her elbows, needing to get a fresh pair of pajamas, but her body wouldn't cooperate further. If Luke hadn't been there she would have washed away the terror with a long, hot shower. He was there, however, separated from her only by a communal bathroom and two closed doors.

Part of her wanted to crawl in bed with him, beg his sympathy, find oblivion in making love until she couldn't think another thought. Until she couldn't picture anything but an imaginary field of flowers misted by a spring shower—anything other than what she'd just seen again in the dreams she'd thought were long gone.

It hadn't worked before, though, so why should it this time? If anything, it would probably be worse, because of who and what Lucas Walker was. Would always be. She had no fantasies about him changing. Part of his charm, albeit questionable sometimes, was his unapologetic belief in himself. It's true he was searching to find a new place in the world now, but nothing stood in the way of his accomplishing that goal. He would have a normal life. She didn't doubt it for a minute.

Oh, for the comfort that would bring.

* * *

"I hand each person a card as they pass by?" Luke asked, shuffling the stack Ariel had just handed him.

"That's right. Every time they arrive back at the information table you give them another one. That way they keep track of the number of laps they've gone, around the Center's walking course."

Luke rubbed his jaw. "They can't remember?"

"Shh." She looked around. She'd chosen a job for him that would keep him busy while she attended to other business at the senior citizens center. "No, they can't always remember. They get busy talking and forget."

"Does it even matter?"

"They have goals they set for themselves, Lucas. They want to know if they've reached or exceeded them." She watched him take note of the people milling around, dressed mostly in jogging suits.

"Some of them aren't wearing shoes with enough support," he noted.

"Care to make a donation?" she asked sweetly.

"I might." He cupped her chin and looked hard at her. "I don't believe you caught up on sleep last night."

"You snored. The noise kept me awake."

He let his hand drop. "I do not snore."

"Is that a confirmed fact?"

"Curious about my love life, darlin'? A man who's been engaged twice in this modern age would've been told, don't you think?"

"Good morning, Ariel. Is that a new boyfriend?"

Ariel turned her head by measurable degrees, too stunned by Luke's announcement to focus on the woman who'd approached. Twice? He'd almost been married twice? Well, now, didn't that bit of news put a whole new twist on things. "Um. Oh, uh, Emma, good morning. No, he's not my boyfriend, new or otherwise. This is Luke Walker. He's the president of Titan Athletic Shoes."

"Titan. Just Titan, now," he said, holding out a hand to

the frail, stooped woman. ''We're branching out. Not just shoes anymore.''

''My grandsons like your shoes, young man.''

''I'm glad to hear—''

''Status symbols,'' Emma announced, then clucked her tongue and wagged her head. ''Skewing all the kids' concept about what's important. In my day, we knew the value of a dollar. Didn't waste 'em on high-priced footwear when something practical would do. Had hand-me-downs most of the time, too.''

''Emma! Yoo-hoo, Emma!''

She flitted away to greet her newly arrived friend.

''Well. I guess she put me in my place,'' Luke said, bemusement on his face.

''They speak their minds. It's one of the things I love about them all. Okay, Lucas, you need to take your place. They've started their warm-up stretches.''

Ariel checked on him every so often. Each time, he was smiling more, flirting more. The ladies batted their eyes at him. The men jabbed back in imaginary boxing matches. Only Emma seemed immune, turning her nose up at his efforts.

When Ariel had finished arranging meal deliveries for the Center's housebound members, she joined Luke. The daily walking had ended. He'd pulled up a chair at a round table with a few people, not talking, but listening to them. Intently.

She came up behind him and laid her hand on his shoulder, alerting him that she was there.

Luke pushed back his chair and stood. ''Miz Emma, now don't you go charmin' anyone else the way you did me today. I swear, you wouldn't be able to keep 'em all at bay.''

''Don't get smart with me, young man.''

He leaned over and kissed her cheek. ''I'll take into consideration everything you had to say. I appreciate your honesty.''

Flustered, Emma fumbled with her knitting. ''Maybe there's hope for you yet.''

Luke settled into the driver's seat of Ariel's car a few minutes later. He drummed his fingers on the steering wheel as he pulled away from the curb.

"Don't mind Emma," Ariel said, glancing his way. "She's a chronic complainer."

"But she's right. Kids today have enough on their minds. They shouldn't have to put up with peer pressure over whether or not they're wearin' the right shoes."

"Lucas, we went through it, too."

"But I've contributed to it. Profited from it." He drummed his fingers harder.

"So, what do you propose to do? Erase your football career? Reduce your prices? Shut down your business?"

"Think about it," he said. Not that he hadn't considered the issue before, especially when the marketing department presented a new advertising campaign geared at kids. "You know, this could be a whole new market."

"What could?"

"Seniors. They've got different needs, don't they?"

"Different challenges," Ariel said.

"Yeah. Arthritis, joint replacement, foot problems. Believe me, I can sympathize, even at my age. What if we design a line for seniors? Velcro straps. Better shock absorbency. Designs made to fit an older foot better."

"Affordable."

"Affordable even for Emma." Luke grinned. "Your whole group could star in the ads."

Ariel could picture it. "Emma's grandsons would think she was so cool."

"She'd be a great spokesperson, wouldn't she? We have to do this right away, before any more time passes. I'm gonna start on it first thing when I get back to the office."

Ariel smiled to herself. All it took was personal involvement, getting people to really look at others, to see them as individuals. That's the way change came about. Luke had just taken a big leap of awareness. He'd find the rewards waiting, just as she had.

Satisfied, she closed her eyes and rested the final few blocks to the youth center.

Four

Chase Ryan, administrator of the Wilson Buckley Youth Center, was the meanest-looking person Ariel knew. In the three years she'd known him, she hadn't once seen him smile. His granite face hewn in a perpetual scowl, he could turn the toughest, most foul-mouthed teenager into a model of good manners with just a look. Every kid who came to the Center learned fast that the soft-spoken man meant business. Oh, he gave second chances—once—but he had no tolerance for people, young or old, who didn't learn from their mistakes.

Ariel and Chase coexisted peacefully because each respected the way the other worked—Ariel with warmth and friendliness, Chase with uncompromising expectations. She wondered how Luke and Chase would get along.

When Ariel and Luke stepped into the Center, they almost crashed into Chase, who had a giggling child tucked like a football under each arm.

"Ariel," he said without expression.

"It's the mermaid," the three-year-old boy under his arm shouted. "Hi, Mermaid."

"Jacob. What's happening?" She high-fived both kids, then looked at the man holding them again. "Chase, this is Luke Walker. Chase Ryan."

Chase nodded. His gaze bore into Luke's. "Thanks for stepping in. It made a big difference." He hitched the kids a little higher and walked toward the classroom the preschoolers used.

"Rules with an iron fist, I'll bet," Luke commented to Ariel.

"You'd be surprised. He's complicated, but he grows on you. Let's head into the gym and see how they're doing setting up the equipment for Saturday."

"Why'd the boy call you Mermaid?" Luke asked as they walked.

"Because of my name." At his blank expression, she added, "*The Little Mermaid?*" Still no response. "The Disney movie?"

"Guess I've been out of touch," he said.

"Don't *you* ever get teased, Luke *Sky*walker?"

"Not more than once. My parents certainly didn't choose my name knowing it'd be some famous character. I'm guessin' yours didn't pick your name because of a fictional mermaid."

"My parents didn't choose the name at all. Oh, there's Sam and Marguerite. They beat us here."

Luke stopped her from moving all the way into the cavernous gymnasium. "Hold on, there. What do you mean your parents didn't choose your name?"

"It doesn't matter."

It mattered. Something flashed in her eyes before she turned and walked away, although her tone of voice hadn't conveyed it. Something she could control by pretending it wasn't of consequence.

He watched her hug Sam and Marguerite, a gesture as natural as breathing, he realized. Which meant that when she'd hugged him last night, he'd placed too much importance on the act. Every time he thought he had her figured out, his assumptions got turned upside down.

The hours slipped by. Luke read reports, consulted with Sam and Chase, asked questions and offered advice, although he was constantly distracted by Ariel as she helped erect the Couch Potatoes equipment. He couldn't keep his gaze off her for longer than a few minutes at a time. She was light on her feet, musical in her laugh, spirited in her enthusiasm.

At some point she pulled her hair into a ponytail, revealing her makeup-free face, her delicate features. She was pretty, in a wholesome, natural kind of way, he decided. And she was complicated enough to be interesting. Kids loved her. Seniors loved her.

Yep. This time he'd chosen the right woman for the right reasons. Twenty-seven was a good age for marriage. She'd be ready to settle down.

"Afraid to get your hands dirty?" Ariel asked, coming up to him as he leaned on a table and stared at the floor plan for the athletic event. Chase stood beside him, his arms crossed.

Luke smiled lazily. "Well, now, Ariel, we each have our callin'. Yours would seem to be in manual labor."

"And yours would be in...?"

"Supervisin'."

"You do it well."

He grinned. "Thanks, darlin'."

"I thought you'd like to know the Titan gear has arrived. Marguerite is checking the shipment against the order sheet. And I've got to head out to deliver some meals. I'll swing back and pick you up around seven or so, we can grab a quick bite to eat, then I've got to check in at the community center about the dinner-dance."

"I'll go with you."

"I suppose it'd be useless to argue with you," she said after a moment.

"Luke Walker, as I live and breathe!"

An elegant, thirtyish woman strode across the gym, high heels in hand.

Luke swallowed. Hell. Judith Abrams, one of the two lawyers on his wife list. What was she doing here?

"Hi, Chase," she said as she reached them. "Ariel. I'm glad you're here, too. I need to talk to you."

Luke watched the women hug. This wasn't good. Not good at all.

"Judith." He offered his hand.

"I don't rate a hug?" she asking, taking one.

Over her shoulder he saw Ariel frown slightly.

"So, what's this I hear about you wife hunting?" Judith asked.

Luke coughed, hiding his surprise. How could she know? He didn't dare glance Ariel's way. "I don't know what you're talkin' about, Judith."

"I saw Cassie interview you on the eleven-o'clock news last month. You said—"

"It was a joke."

"What was?" Ariel asked.

Judith didn't take her eyes off Luke. He could tell she was analyzing the situation, a skill at which she excelled.

"Cassie's a sportscaster on Channel Eight, Ariel," Judith said. "You know how they always ask the MVP of the Super Bowl at the end of the game what he's going to do now, and he always says he's going to Disneyland?"

Ariel looked a little embarrassed. "I've never seen a Super Bowl game," she admitted.

Judith turned to look at her then. "You're kidding? Well, they do. Anyway, Cassie was doing a piece on Luke's retirement. She said since he couldn't go to Disneyland this year— You did know he was MVP last year, right?"

"Um, yeah. I heard that."

"When Cassie asked what his plans were, he said maybe he'd find himself a little woman and settle down."

"'A little woman'?" Ariel repeated, looking at Luke in disbelief. "You said that? 'A little woman'?"

"It was a joke," he insisted, feeling sweat bead on his forehead. "Thanks, Judith. I'd been tryin' to live that one down."

"Hey, what are friends for? I heard you were helping out here at the Center. I think it's great."

"What are you doing here?" he asked, ignoring Ariel's bewildered expression.

"I'm the attorney for the Angel Foundation." She hefted her briefcase. "And I've got some papers for you, Ariel. You don't have to sign them today, though. Just take them home and look them over."

"Okay. Come with me while I wash my hands. I've got to pick up the meals and get them delivered."

Luke watched them walk across the gym. Ariel didn't take a straight path, of course, but one that brought her in contact with most of the people working so that she could make a comment, pat a shoulder and give a quick hug, talking with Judith the whole way. At one point she glanced back at him and grinned. He could only imagine what Judith was telling her. They'd dated now and then when she was between relationships. Nothing serious ever developed, but he liked her enough to put her on the list. Seeing the two women side by side, though…

When he realized his gaze had settled on Ariel's hips and was lingering appreciatively, he tossed his pencil on the table and turned to Chase. "If you make that switch, you'll have more room for the long jump. A larger sand pit will mean less chance for injury."

"Done. Thanks." Chase glanced at the doorway the women had just strolled through.

Luke scratched his head. Ariel baffled him as much as any woman had. More, even. Comfortable in a man's company, he spoke his thoughts aloud to Chase. "Ariel's amazing. Tireless."

"Yeah. This place would've folded without her."

"Without the Angel Foundation, anyway," Luke said.

"Same thing."

"Is it?"

Chase shrugged. "She's on a mission."

"Makes me wonder what she's running from."

An easy silence settled between the men.

"Stop by later and see the place in action when school's out," Chase said after a bit. "The kids know about you. Maybe you could give them a few pointers."

Luke's knee twinged at the thought. "If the unstoppable Miz Minx can squeeze it into our schedule, I'll do that." He shoved some papers into his briefcase as he watched Ariel jog toward him across the gymnasium, waving goodbye to people as she went. She was alone. For a second, just a second, he thought both her feet actually left the ground, as if wings lifted her.

Earth angel. The description was dead-on accurate.

They said goodbye to Chase and walked toward the exit.

"Judith told me a delightful tale about a certain New Year's Eve party a couple of years back," Ariel said, a smile forming. She watched resignation settle on his face.

"Well, now, if you know Judith, you know she's got a wicked sense of humor. And she's a helluva storyteller. That's why she's such a good lawyer."

"Are you saying that you *didn't* serenade the mayor then moon him when he came to the window?"

"You have to know the whole story, darlin'. He'd insulted our quarterback. We couldn't take that lyin' down."

"Just standin' up," she teased. "Naked."

"Just for a second. And just our butts. Besides, there were probably fifteen of us. It wasn't personal between him and me."

"Did he recognize you?"

"It's safe to say he knew who was salutin' him."

She looped her arm through his and rested her cheek against his arm. "I wish I'd been there."

"You can have a free look, if you want."

She laughed. "I was thinking more that I would've liked

to have seen the mayor's reaction, but I wouldn't mind a private showing.'' She looked up at him and smiled slowly.

He took it all back. She was a devil in disguise. No doubt about it.

''It's a tax deduction for the restaurant,'' Ariel said over Luke's laughter. They pulled away from the curb, the back of her car loaded with the hot and cold food carriers they'd just picked up. She'd taken over the driving because she knew her own route. Like most men, he didn't like being a passenger, however.

''Leave it to you, darlin'. Your shut-ins get supper from some fancy French restaurant that even I would think twice about goin' to, given the eye-poppin' prices on the menu.''

''And just because these people couldn't afford it, means they don't appreciate it?''

''Now, I didn't say that.''

''I've lined up twenty restaurants willing to prepare meals, so they aren't having to do it all that often. And the recipients are grateful, Lucas.''

''Don't you go gettin' that prissy look, Ariel. I admire what you've done. Truly I do.'' He saw her hands relax on the steering wheel. ''It's real simple for people to make cash donations to anonymous causes. I'm guilty of it myself. You make it personal. That's commendable.''

''Sorry. I'm a little defensive. It's really just a small dent in what's needed.'' She pulled into a driveway. ''And I don't do it for any glory.''

''I can see that, darlin'. You need to give as much as they need to receive.''

Their gazes met and held.

At her silence, he prodded her. ''Do you know why?''

''It makes me feel good.''

''And?''

''That's enough, isn't it?'' She turned off the ignition and pulled up the door handle. ''You can stay in the car or you can help. It's up to you.''

"I'll help."

The afternoon was an education for Luke. They delivered meals to fifteen seniors who weren't able to cook for themselves. At each stop, Ariel spent about ten minutes setting up the meal, asking and answering questions, offering a human touch.

Some of the apartments, or boarding house rooms, were so run-down Luke thought they should be condemned. Most were sparsely decorated, excruciatingly neat. Television was a constant companion. Cats frequently held court.

He thought of his grandparents, living comfortably in their home in the mountains, able to afford good medical care, still able to fend for themselves, although they had slowed down some.

"This is the last stop," Ariel said as she turned off the car. "I don't see a parking place except this one, which is illegal. Would you mind staying with the car in case someone decides to ticket me?"

Luke started to say yes, then he saw her fidget. She wouldn't look at him, either. What was different about this house? This shut-in?

"I'll pay the fine, if you get one," he said amiably as he opened his door and stepped out.

She met him at the back of the car. "Really, Lucas, it's okay. I can manage. And I'm more worried about being towed, actually."

"I'll keep my eyes peeled this way." He slid the remaining cartons from the carriers, then stepped onto the sidewalk and awaited her. She followed more slowly.

When she reached him, she put a hand on his arm. "This one isn't from the senior center."

"Oh?"

"In fact, Jan is only thirty-two."

He waited.

"She has AIDS, Lucas. And she's in the advanced stages. You need to know, in case that makes a difference."

"Exactly what kind of difference, Ariel?"

"It isn't easy. I've known her for years, before she began to deteriorate so drastically. I remember what a vibrant woman she was. You'll see only what she is now."

"I'll try not to show my revulsion."

Ariel's head snapped back at his sarcasm. She analyzed his expression. "I've offended you," she said.

"Damn right you've offended me."

"I'm sor—"

"Apology accepted," he said abruptly. "Lead the way."

As Ariel prepared the food tray a few minutes later, Luke spoke with Jan, listened to her, laughed at her jokes and held her hand.

Held her hand. Ariel almost cried into the soup she'd just reheated. What in the world was she going to do with him? He kept surprising her, kept revealing layers of his personality that appealed to her. It was really too bad that he had so many strikes against him, as well.

The dream returned, this time in Technicolor. Ariel sat straight up, gasping for breath, clawing the air, clinging to nothing. An acrid scent stung her nostrils. As taut as a harp string, she sat paralyzed until reality wrapped a shawl around her, welcoming her back to her own bedroom and the soothing bowl of rose-scented potpourri on her nightstand.

Rubbing her face with her hands, she cursed the cause of the dream's return. Undoubtedly, he lay sleeping dreamlessly after their long day, a day that hadn't ended until hours after they'd left Jan's place. His knee seemed to be bothering him a lot as they'd climbed the stairs to Ariel's apartment around ten-thirty, although he denied it. Tomorrow would be more of the same running around and planning, followed by the double dose of events the next day. He probably needed to stay put and rest, but undoubtedly he wouldn't, just as she needed to sleep, and couldn't.

A cup of warm cocoa would help, she decided. She'd go put a mug in the microwave then change her pajamas while she waited for it to heat.

Ariel inched open her bedroom door. She tiptoed across the living room and into the kitchen. Realizing the microwave would beep when she set the time, then beep again when the cocoa was done, she decided to use a pan. The room lit only by the open refrigerator, she added instant hot chocolate mix to milk and set the pan on the stove. She pushed the refrigerator door shut and turned to go back to her room.

"Can't sleep?"

Startled, she grabbed the nearest counter, her fingernails digging uselessly against the Formica. "What are you doing up, Lucas?"

"Same thing you are, I suspect." He flipped on a light. "Gettin' something to drink. What the—" He grabbed her by the shoulders. "What the hell happened to you?"

She lifted her chin. "Hot flashes."

Luke could see that she was embarrassed, but he didn't have a clue whether she was serious. What did he know of female problems? Hot flashes supposedly came with the change of life. She couldn't be going through menopause at her age, could she?

"What's goin' on, Ariel?"

"I told you." She pulled away. "I'll be back in a minute. If you want hot chocolate, add some to what's in the pan."

He let her go because he was confused, but not before noticing how he could almost see her body beneath her clinging pajamas. Small, high breasts, a slender torso, hand-spanning waist, narrow hips. Long legs—those he remembered from the cruise. He'd always been an admirer of long, shapely—

With a muttered curse, he grabbed the milk carton from the refrigerator and added some to the pan, then extra chocolate. He swiped a hand down his face. Hell. He'd chosen her because she hadn't made his hormones do the Texas two-step. But when she'd walked away from him...

Well, now, come to think of it, a little sexual attraction was necessary in a marriage, after all. It was good that he desired her—so long as lust didn't take over. Surely their marriage would have no chance of survival if his hormones started rulin' the roost, like before.

Okay. He had it figured out now. Part of wooing himself a wife meant dealin' with the physical aspects as well. He could do that. He could hold her and kiss her, do all those things women needed to feel loved. He'd read plenty of articles about it in women's magazines—his second fiancée had made sure of that, sticking them under his nose every couple of weeks or so. He knew a hot time in bed wasn't enough for women. He'd even learned that about himself.

Idly he stirred the cocoa as it warmed. Ariel must've had a bad dream, he decided. She'd woken up scared, but didn't want to admit it to him. He snorted softly. Stubborn little thing.

He dipped his finger into the hot chocolate, determined it was warm enough, then poured two mugs. He carried them into the living room, leaving the kitchen light on to illuminate the adjacent room slightly. When she joined him, she was wearing sweatpants and a T-shirt, as was he, except that her shirt was long-sleeved.

Luke didn't let her sit at the far end of the couch, but took her hand and pulled her to sit beside him. He passed her the mug. For once she didn't argue with him but sipped her drink in silence. After a few minutes she leaned her head back against the sofa and closed her eyes. He eased the mug from her, set it on the coffee table with his, then settled his arm around her, urging her closer until she lay her head against his chest, one of her arms resting across his stomach, the other tucked between them, against his side.

He could feel the tension flow out of her. Damn, it felt good to know he could do that for her.

Gently, he combed her still-damp hair with his fingers. She sighed as he massaged her scalp.

"Did you have a nightmare?" he asked quietly.

A few heartbeats later, he felt her cheek rub up and down against his chest as she nodded.

"Want to talk about it?"

"Not really."

"Make you feel better."

"I already feel better." She snuggled closer, almost purring. "Your hands are magic."

He continued to massage her scalp. Her head slid down his chest a few inches, then a few more, until she rested against his stomach. He could feel the warmth of her breath, even through his shirt. Her arm now lay across his thighs.

His hormones loudly announced they weren't the slightest bit sleepy.

Hell. Somehow or other he had to get her head where her arm was, or she was going to know how she was affectin' him, all warm and quiet against him again, kind of like a wife should be on a cold winter's night. But nothin' to worry about, he reminded himself. Attraction is important.

"Uh, darlin'?"

"Mmm?"

"Could you scoot down some, maybe put your head on my legs? I can rub your back then, too."

Like a cuddling kitten, she resettled herself sleepily on his thigh, facing away. He breathed carefully as he massaged her back, aware of the delicate bone structure, the smooth muscles and flesh. As he cupped her shoulder she turned her head, telling him wordlessly she wanted her neck rubbed as she burrowed her nose at a point halfway between his knees and his, uh, most wide-awake part of his body.

"Ariel?"

"Mmm?"

"This may be your idea of platonic, darlin', but it sure as hell isn't mine."

Regret settled over him as she pushed herself upright. Her long golden hair was tangled from his touch. Her dark eyes held an expression teetering between exhaustion and primal need. How could a man resist that combination?

He kissed her softly, tenderly, with more care than he'd ever offered a woman. She kissed him back. Hungrily, urgently, with more need than he'd ever felt from a woman. His priorities shifted abruptly.

Forbidden. The word settled in Ariel's mind and took charge. Even his distinctive scent breathed the word to her with every pound of her pulse. She opened her mouth to let a trapped moan escape, and he took instant advantage, pressing harder, drawing more from her than mere cooperation and response. He made her come at him just as hard, pulling back a little at a time, forcing her to take over. She wound her arms around his neck, tugging closer and closer, surprised for only a moment by the needy sounds that came involuntarily from her. Nothing had ever felt as good as this. No one had ever sent her soaring with just a kiss. Oh, more. Please, more, she begged silently.

As if he heard her, he dragged her across his lap as their tongues sought and found each other. His arms enveloped her, beyond comfortable, beyond arousing. She felt his palm come to rest low on her back, then curve over her rear. Her teeth closed on his lower lip lightly as her breath caught. He battled back, maneuvering her lips apart, offering his tongue again. He backed away until their lips barely touched. He said her name like the wind carries a leaf, the sound swirling delicately as he slid his hand around her, coming to rest on her breast, his hesitance evident in the way he kneaded her flesh once, lifted his hand slightly a moment later, then finally settled, as if he couldn't help himself. Her nipple tightened, pressing against his palm.

"Lucas," she breathed, going still, closing her eyes.

He massaged her whole breast gently, then when he brushed the painfully taut crest with his thumb, she jerked so hard in reaction, he grabbed hold of her, literally keeping her from falling off the couch.

"I've got you," he said, his voice gruff.

Ariel dug her fingers into his arms and clenched her teeth, just barely stopping herself from screaming. Those words. Those terrible, wonderful words—"I've got you." Oh, he couldn't know. There wasn't any way he could know what those words meant to her.

Remnants of the dream crawled back. He let her go the instant she asked him to. Putting her clothes to rights, she slid away a couple of feet.

"I'm sorry," she said. "I set the rules, then I didn't adhere to them."

"Some rules are made to be broken. Or were never meant to be made in the first place."

She watched him push his fingers through his hair. She'd felt his arousal as she'd moved against him. She knew she hadn't been fair. "Maybe," she said. "Regardless, I apologize."

"Accepted. Are you feelin' better?"

"Yes." After a minute of not talking, they stood simultaneously and headed to their bedrooms. She flipped on the light switch just inside her door, then turned back to him. "I didn't get to talk to you about something I've been wondering about, but I guess it's too late now. Maybe tomorrow."

He leaned against the frame, his arms crossed. "About what?"

She rubbed her nose. "Um, I was kind of curious about what you and Judith were talking about. You know, about settling down."

"What about it? It was a joke."

"Was it really?"

"I'm not sayin' the thought hasn't crossed my mind. I'm thirty-four, after all."

She looked him straight in the eye. "Personally, I have no plans to get married."

He didn't even blink. "No?"

"And I'm not having children."

"You'd be a great mother."

"I don't have time for a family. There's still so much to do." He hadn't moved an inch. Hadn't shifted. Hadn't changed his facial expression. She realized she'd made a big mistake. He didn't have marriage to her in mind. An affair, maybe. But not marriage. Well. Could she have embarrassed herself any more than this?

"Um, okay. I just wondered. Good night, Lucas."

When she shut the door, he still hadn't budged. Hadn't said good-night. He just smiled at her. A quirky, *egotistical* half smile that was way too self-satisfied.

He'd somehow turned her own words against her. Darned if she knew how, or why, or what the truth was anymore. She knew only that he'd maintained control while she'd babbled like an idiot.

Damn the man, anyway.

Five

Funny how childhood memories could creep up on a person, Luke thought. He stared out of Ariel's living room window, watching the lights across the bay come on one by one as night descended. They'd been home half an hour from the day-long Couch Potatoes event. She was showering before dressing for the dinner-dance. He was waiting his turn, icing his knee—and thinking.

He'd seen himself as a child a hundred times today at the Center. Had remembered his own desperate need for attention and recognition. He differed from many of the kids at the event today only because he'd had the luxury of having both parents around.

Proximity must count for something. And they'd never been cruel to him, except for a bewildering lack of attention. Still—if they'd thought to give him a brother or sister, at least he wouldn't have felt so alone so much of the time.

Luke lifted the ice pack and looked at his knee. After the long day standing and walking, his knee throbbed in rhythm with his pulse, the pain unrelenting. The swelling had subsided a little, though, and he hoped Ariel would stay in the shower a few more minutes.

Soothed by the view out her window, he thought back to when he'd first discovered football—and a whole new family bond. The family members changed frequently, including the parental role, but the needs filled by the game itself were enough—camaraderie, team play, hard work resulting in personal satisfaction. Being appreciated. Achieving success, which was always the measure of a man. It all counted. Now it was all gone. And he had to live with it—and achieve new successes. The road ahead was more difficult than the one he'd walked until now.

When the shower water stopped, he eased off the couch and hobbled into the kitchen before Ariel caught him icing his knee. He ran hot water to melt the ice cubes, trashed the plastic bag, dried his leg with a couple of swipes of a dish towel, then pulled on sweatpants over his shorts, all the while considering the fact that Ariel knew every child at the Center. Obviously she spent a lot more time there than he'd guessed. She had no social life whatsoever. Her life centered around her projects.

She needed him. That's all there was to it.

He stifled a groan as he left the kitchen. He was paying for his pride of having left his crutches at home, as well as putting off the surgery. Except that he'd be on crutches now, anyway, if he'd gone through with the operation. But at least his reason for not dancing would be apparent. Instead he would have to make up excuses. The pain killer was just now starting to take hold. He could probably manage her stairs by the time they left, and the first couple of hours beyond that.

"Bathroom's all yours," she called out from behind her bedroom door.

He heard her hair dryer come on just as he turned the hot water knob. The sounds of daily living, as it should be—like some old married couple. Comforted by the thought, he ducked his head under the hot spray and sighed.

Forty-five minutes later he slipped his wallet into his back pocket, checked the knot on his tie once more, then slid his jacket on. He'd taken his time getting ready, figuring she wouldn't be done much before the scheduled time of departure. He was right about that, which made him smile.

He felt married already, could predict almost everything about her. In the days he'd spent with her, he'd come to the conclusion she could run a home or a business, or probably even a battleship, equally well. She set everyone at ease with her smile, her genuine show of interest, her competence. Competence? It was an unusual trait to admire, perhaps, but he did. His life would require her competence as much as his own. They would travel extensively, entertain constantly.

Ready to go, he wandered into the living room.

She opened her door a crack. "I'll be done in two minutes."

"Take your time. We've got ten minutes or so." Damn, he liked this…this *sharing* with her. Sharing space, sharing conversation, sharing lives. It was so easy.

Her bedroom door opened and she moved into the room. He let out a long whistle as he eyed her from her golden blond, upswept hair to her body-defining long black gown, with its high neckline, long sleeves and simple design. She seemed a foot taller, although her high heels probably added only three inches or so. "Well, look at you, darlin'. Don't you look like some kinda movie star."

Ariel returned the compliment, anticipating the evening ahead. She couldn't wait to dance with him, to be in his arms for a whole song or two or three, or more.

"Let me grab my shawl, then we can go," she said, turning toward the coat closet, giving him a different view, where a soft U-shaped drape of fabric fell from her shoulders to her waist, leaving her back bare. A leg-revealing slit teased his attention from her mid-thigh all the way down to her hem.

When she turned around, her shawl clutched in her fist, she caught the look of tension on his face, the darkening of his deep blue eyes to almost black, the furrowing of his brow, as if he were seeing her for the first time and didn't know what to make of her.

She set her beaded bag on the shelf below a wall mirror and started to wrap her shawl around her.

"That's my privilege, I believe," he said.

She faced the mirror as he came up behind her and took the garment, then folded it over his arm instead. His gaze on hers in the mirror, he traced the scoop of fabric down her back, his fingertips brushing her flesh in hot, tempting strokes.

"You should be wearin' some kinda warnin' sign, darlin'. Dangerous curves ahead."

At his touch, her nipples drew tight beneath the soft, clingy fabric. She saw his gaze shift downward to watch until they'd hardened under his scrutiny. He lowered his head. His lips grazed her neck. She tipped her head back and moaned softly.

She held her breath as he slid an arm around her, splayed his large hand across her stomach. When he spread his fingers wide, his thumb pillowed her left breast, growing heavy and sensitive with arousal. The tip of his little finger reached low enough to tease her into a hard throb of response, faster than light, quicker than sound.

She lifted her arms, curved them behind her, over his shoulders, arching her body upward, seeking…more, something more than this tight, about-to-explode need that radiated through her. He brought his hips against her, aligning his aroused flesh with her buttocks, pressing close, tempting her with his blatant response. She savored the reflection in the mirror of the mingling black and white and flesh tones of their clothes and bodies, the matching streaks of gold in their hair, the hard, bright edge of arousal glittering in their eyes.

"What exactly are you wearin' under this bit of temptation, darlin'?"

"You tell me."

He responded to her challenge with a personal investigation—very personal. He cupped her breasts, lifting them a little higher, caressing the taut peaks until need shot straight to the heart of her femininity.

"You draw me to you like some kinda power source I can't control." His fingers spread wide, he pushed his hands down her body, moseying over every inch, measuring each rib, dipping into the indentation of her navel. He blanketed his hands over her abdomen like a husband does over a wife's pregnant belly.

Ever so slowly his fingertips moved to the center, tracing the apex where her thighs met. He slid a foot between hers, nudging her legs apart. Shocked by the unfamiliar expression she saw on her own face, she arched her back and closed her eyes, ignoring the wanton woman she didn't recognize. She let herself enjoy the sensations, instead, as he pressed the heel of his hand against her and rubbed, a circular motion building in power that was mirrored inside her.

She shifted back and forth, needing…something. Friction crackled. She heard herself make strange, low sounds, and wondered whether she was shocked or embarrassed by them. She could feel the impending explosion, so close. So very close. Just a tiny bit more pressure, then—

"Feels like you under there, Ariel. And only you," he said, releasing her.

She opened her eyes. He watched her, still, his features sharply defined, his face almost as flushed as hers.

Somehow words made their way past the wild need that had built within her with his inquiring touch and flattering gaze. She'd known he'd be a good lover. A generous lover. Tonight. Definitely tonight. If she lasted that long. "Give the man a gold star," she said, trying to act as casually as Luke.

He picked up her shawl from the floor, where it had fallen early on. He wrapped it around her. "Pretty good wind swirlin' out there. Could make you cold in places you've never been cold before."

"I'll take my chances." She turned around and ran her palms down his lapels. She wanted that image planted in his head all night—thoughts of her wearing nothing beneath the dress but thigh-high stockings. She had no intention of dancing with anyone but Luke tonight, so no one else would ever know. They only had tonight left. After the Super Bowl tomorrow, he'd fly back to Nevada. And somehow her life had to go on as before.

She wanted memories of tonight with him—dancing, teasing, making love. It had been a long, long time since she'd been attracted to a man, and never like this. Never this powerfully.

It was dangerous. She knew that. And she was risking so much. If they'd had more time together, she would have tried to draw it out longer, but time was short and she was needy. And so, she believed, was he.

Luke watched Ariel laugh at something Chase Ryan said. They sat at a table next to the stage and opened the bid envelopes for the silent auction, tallying the results, with Sam and Marguerite representing Titan's promised public involvement. You aren't jealous, Luke told himself for the third time. Chase doesn't know she isn't wearin' a blasted thing under her dress. Of course, any man with an average store of testosterone might guess just by lookin'. But he wouldn't know for sure without touching. As Luke had.

Hell. So much for no lustful thoughts of Ariel. Who would've guessed that underneath that angelic facade lurked such a temptress? She always seemed so…wholesome. He hadn't had much experience with wholesome women. Obviously he'd been missing something.

For the first time he wondered about her past. More to the point, her love life. She'd certainly responded to him, but she hadn't instigated anything herself. How was he supposed to interpret that?

The hall of the community center was too noisy for any serious contemplation of the subject, so he gave it up. The six-piece band played show tunes as dessert plates were cleared. White-jacketed waiters and waitresses served coffee, tea and champagne as the guests awaited the results of the auction before Luke personally auctioned off one last item—the jersey he'd worn during last year's Super Bowl, when he'd been named Most Valuable Player.

He hoped it would pull in enough money to make his sacrifice worthwhile, and enough not to be embarrassed by a piddling amount.

A local radio host, emcee for the evening, walked onto the stage and spoke into the microphone, asking for attention. He introduced a couple of speakers, who thanked everyone for the success of the day, then the auction winners were announced and the items distributed to applause and jeers and impromptu negotiations from the floor.

Luke watched Ariel as she remained seated at the business table. No one introduced her, nor was she thanked in either of the speeches by the Center's supporters. He spotted Chase leaning against a wall and approached him.

"Making a lot of money tonight," Luke said.

"Yeah. More than we hoped, thanks to you."

Luke stuck his hands in his pockets. "I'm curious why Ariel hasn't been thanked publicly. She's the one who's done the most, I'd say."

Chase's expression turned more serious than usual. He contemplated Luke in silence for almost half a minute. "Ariel stays out of the limelight."

"You mean it's her choice?"

"No one is slighting her, Luke. She insists on no recognition."

"Why?"

Chase shrugged.

Luke considered this information, adding it to what else he knew of her. Everything she did was strictly behind the scenes. Everything. Why? She should be thanked, at least.

"Don't do it, Luke."

"Do what?"

"Don't recognize her publicly. She'll never forgive you."

"What makes you think—" Luke frowned. It really bothered him that Chase knew her better than he did, particularly when he'd just this evening come to the conclusion that he could predict everything about her.

"Ladies and gentlemen," the deejay said, his voice booming. "Before we give you the final tally for the night, we've got one last item up for bid. A public bid, this time. You all know Luke Walker of our own San Francisco Gold Dusters. Let's give Luke a warm welcome as he joins me up here, then you can get out your checkbooks."

Luke had made his way onto stages and platforms since he was seventeen years old when his athletic skills had started bringing him fame. He'd never felt as uncomfortable as he did this time. His career was over. Over. Didn't they understand that? They should be auctioning off something of Mark Malone's. He was the new star of the team. He'd taken them to the Super Bowl this year.

He glanced Ariel's way, and she smiled at him, a smile just for him, something different from the warm gesture she offered everyone else. He didn't know how it was different. It just was. There were stars in her eyes, too, but not like those of an idolizing fan. More like some tender I-know-you-Lucas-Walker sparkle that warmed him inside out. Like everyone else, she was applauding, the motion making her breasts—

Hell. He swallowed. Keep your mind on business, Luke.

The requisite introduction followed, a long, glorified list of his professional accomplishments. He tried not to squirm. He'd been doing his best to put that part of his life behind him, while everyone else kept wanting to remind him of it. He needed to go forward, toward the expansion of Titan, a plan he'd had since he was twenty-two. Toward marriage. Toward fatherhood. Life. Real life.

The deejay opened the bidding at five hundred dollars, and

it climbed to five thousand dollars before anyone could draw three breaths.

"Well, heck," Luke drawled. "I'll pay six thousand to keep it. Come on, folks. These kids are countin' on you."

"I'll bid seven thousand dollars, if you'll also model it, Luke," a woman in the front called out.

Silence came first, then murmurs and laughter.

He grinned. "Without shoulder pads underneath, you'd be *real* disappointed, ma'am."

A woman seated in the middle of the room raised the shoulder pads she'd won in the silent auction. "Here y'go, Luke. You can borrow these."

He hated this. He really hated this.

"Eight thousand if you'll take off your shirt and put on the gear right now," the woman down front shouted.

Beefcake. That's all he was. He kept some kind of smile on his face. His gaze swept the room, not really seeing anyone's face in particular, just a patchwork quilt of anticipation. Then he zeroed in on Ariel. Tell me what to do, here? he asked her silently.

Ariel raised her hand. "Nine thousand. And he can keep his shirt on."

That earned her a glare from the woman doing the bidding, who then drummed her fingers on the table a few times. "Ten thousand, including a dance, Luke."

Ariel didn't up her bid. No one else added to it. Sold to the lady in red.

The band started up again, a tune intended to draw people onto the dance floor. Luke hand-delivered the jersey to the woman. Someone else collected her check. She pulled the jersey over her head and passed him a pen.

"Sign it right here, will you, Luke? On the top of the eight."

The top of the eight was cushioned by a substantial breast. He glanced from it to her face. Suddenly her teeth looked as pointed as a shark's. He knew that twenty feet away Ariel watched. In the old days—even as recently as six months ago—he might have scrawled his name leisurely right where the woman asked.

But those days were long behind him. Plus Miz Wholesome was watching. He didn't want to disappoint her—or himself.

He offered a polite smile to the woman for her generosity, then he grabbed the jersey at the shoulder and tugged it upward, where he could sign it against her collarbone.

"You don't remember me, do you, Luke?"

Luke hesitated, the pen clenched between his fingers. "I'm sorry. I don't—"

"I sold your house for you a few months ago."

Aw, hell. She was on his damned wife list, he realized. The Realtor. "Well, 'course I remember you." What was her name? Oh, yeah. "Madeline. Fastest home sale on record. It slipped my mind with all the confusion tonight. Forgive me?"

She pouted. "Maybe."

He signed the jersey, taking care not to touch her inappropriately, although she moved at some point so that the heel of his hand bumped her breast. He clenched his teeth. Figuring the song was half-over, he started dancing with her.

She pulled herself closer as they moved to the music. "How about dinner sometime, Luke?"

"I'm kinda involved, Madeline."

"Oh. How disappointing. Ten thousand dollars—"

"For the Wilson Buckley Youth Center. And we appreciate your generosity. Come tax time, I hope you remember us fondly." He kissed her cheek in some sort of compensation as the music stopped, then he turned away and walked straight to Ariel.

"Would you like to dance?" he asked, extending his hand as the band segued into a slower song.

"I would be honored."

They danced in comfortable silence. He ignored his knee as it tried to remind him that it couldn't be ignored for much longer. "Don't laugh, but I felt cheap up there," he said at last.

"I could tell." She rested her head against his shoulder as he enveloped her with both arms and, instead of dancing, just sort of moved with her.

"What would you have done if she hadn't upped the bid that last time?" he asked.

"Had myself a very expensive nightshirt."

Luke's laugh started soft and turned warm. "Well, thanks for rescuin' me."

"She had more than charity on her mind."

"I believe she did." If he didn't sit down soon, he was going to pass out. His doctor was going to blister his ears with a stinging lecture. She'd been ticked off enough when he'd delayed the surgery for two weeks, but he'd obviously damaged his knee further with all he'd done the past few days. And he'd seen so many players get hooked on pain pills that he tried to go as long as possible between doses. But, man, he needed double strength tonight.

"How long until we can make a graceful exit?" he asked Ariel as the song ended.

"Not for a couple of hours, at least."

They walked to the table and took their seats. He stretched out his leg, wishing he could rest his foot on another chair. "You just give me the sign, and I'll get the car," he said. "The sooner—"

"Luke!"

He turned when his name was called. Hell. Another woman from his stupid wife list. The television sportscaster. He plastered on a smile as she descended, cameraman in tow, and a newspaper reporter hot on her heels. "Hey, there, Cassie. How're you doin'?"

"Where have you been, Luke? Everyone figured you'd be hanging around this week, encouraging the Dusters, but then no sign of you. I couldn't believe it when I got a call that you were here tonight. What's going on?"

He turned toward Ariel but found her seat empty and no

sign of her in the vicinity. He sighed inwardly. She'd left him to face the media tigress alone.

"We're bein' followed."

Ariel looked over her shoulder. She saw the headlights of another car.

"They've been behind us since we left the dance," Luke said, glancing at the rearview mirror again. "I think it's the reporter who arrived at the same time as Cassie. I made the mistake of not talkin' with him."

"Great."

"I'm sorry about tonight, Ariel. Someone tipped 'em off that I was there."

"I probably should've alerted the media myself. The Center can always use publicity, but I figured since we were sold out already, it wouldn't make any difference." *I was selfish. I wanted to dance with you tonight, without a lot of public scrutiny. I only got one dance before—*

"I'm glad you didn't contact the press. Would've turned into a circus a lot earlier, and it wouldn't have been nearly as much fun." He looked in the mirror again. "Now what? He's gonna follow us home."

"I don't have any experience with this kind of thing. You tell me."

"Chances are he'll park outside your apartment, waitin' to see if I spend the night. He'll check the address to see who lives there. Reporters are pretty mule-headed. You could be all over the papers tomorrow." He frowned. "I believe this calls for a little diversionary tactic."

"How? You mean, keep driving until you lose him?"

"Nope. I've learned it's better to face 'em head-on. I'll walk you to your door, then leave, if you don't mind my takin' your car. I'll come back after I've dealt with him. That okay with you?"

So much for our last night together, she thought. "How long will you be gone?"

"An hour. Two, tops." He curved his hand over hers, clenched in her lap. "I'm really sorry about this, darlin'."

She'd known. Oh, she'd known and let herself forget how much of a public figure he was. An admired man. A hero to some. She'd known and she'd ignored it, because he intrigued her more than any man had. Ever.

"It's all right, Lucas. Really." She smiled at him. "Thank you for making this day so successful for the Center. The money will be well spent."

"Good. You can count on Titan's continued involvement, too. I like what I see happening there. Without Chase, though, I'm not sure the standards would be maintained." He turned the corner of Ariel's street, pulled up in front of her building and turned off the engine.

"Chase isn't going anywhere. The Center's his whole life."

"You ever date him?"

The question was asked casually, but Ariel detected something else. She would have been flippant, except that she was pretty sure she heard jealousy behind his words, and the last thing she wanted was for him to feel insecure about her. "No. Chase and I are too much alike."

His silence seemed to indicate that he accepted her answer.

"Just as I thought. The car pulled over, too," he said.

They opened their doors and slid out, then didn't touch as they climbed the stairs to her duplex.

"Don't wait up," he said. "I'll see you in the morning."

Ariel shut the door behind herself. *Don't wait up.* What was he, superhuman? She wanted him so much she ached just thinking about it. And he had seemed to want her earlier. What was the truth?

Almost an hour passed before she was ready for bed. She hung up her dress with care, cleansed her face free of makeup, brushed out her hair. She was exhausted, but she knew sleep would elude her until Luke was back. She took a hot bath, dusted herself with powder, then donned a seafoam green, lacy gown she'd never worn before. The low neckline barely covered her nipples, the translucent fabric revealing shadows of what lay below.

She turned on her bedside light and glanced at the clock. Almost midnight. They didn't have to leave for the stadium tomorrow until noon, which meant they could stay up for another couple of hours and still get a whole night's sleep. She pulled a box of condoms from her dresser drawer and put one packet on the nightstand, under the box of tissues there, not wanting to be obvious. Maybe he had a favorite kind that he would provide.

She turned on her electric blanket to warm the sheets, debated about where she should wait for him—in the living room or in bed?—added more condoms hopefully to the one in hiding, and headed toward the kitchen, intending to brew some tea. The front door opened as she stepped into the living room. Only the light from her bedroom behind her illuminated the room.

He shut the door and rested against it, watching her. She strolled toward him.

"All taken care of?" she asked.

"Yep."

"What'd you do?"

"Went to Sam and Marguerite's hotel. The reporter figured I was a guest there. I gave him a couple of quotes, then hung out in Sam and Marguerite's suite for an hour."

His tie was gone, his shirt unbuttoned to mid-chest. She flattened her hands on his lapels when she came up to him. Smoke clung to him, a scent she didn't find nearly as unpleasant as she had before. She separated the shirt with her hands, sliding her palms over the contours of his chest, discovering a soft mat of hair, and skin cold from the winter night. She pressed her lips to the tempting spot over his heart as she tugged his shirt loose from his waistband.

"Ariel?"

"Hmm?"

"Uh, darlin', I have to be honest here."

She froze. Now what? A rejection? Why was it she constantly made a fool of herself with him? She took a step back, then another.

''My knee hurts so much I can't even think straight. I pushed myself, and I'm payin' for it, big-time. If I don't get a pain pill in me right away, you're gonna think you're livin' with some kind of wild animal.''

As excuses went, it was original, Ariel thought. She walked away before she uttered a sarcastic reply.

''I'm sorry,'' he said behind her. ''I wouldn't be any good to you tonight.''

''Good night, Lucas.''

Luke stumbled around in the dark when she shut her door. Swearing as he felt for objects in his path, he finally grasped the doorknob to his bedroom and flipped on the switch. Great. Sam and Marguerite were mad at him for dropping by unannounced. He'd passed the time there by icing his knee and wishing for something stronger than the over-the-counter pain relievers Marguerite had offered. Now Ariel was ticked off, too.

Nothing was going right for him. Women from his wife list popped up. His knee was probably damaged beyond repair now. Ariel was furious. Or hurt. Or both. And he still had to get through the game tomorrow.

He wanted to go home. Back to the life he was creating for himself.

Hell, who was he kidding? He wanted sympathy. Ariel's sympathy.

He tossed his jacket onto the bed, stripped to his boxer shorts, dumped a pill in his hand and limped into the bathroom to get some water. Glaring at the door to her bedroom, he downed the medication.

Before he could talk himself out of it, he flung open her door and hobbled in. The bathroom light spotlighted her. She bolted upright. As he reached her bed and plopped onto it, he leaned forward to turn on her bedside lamp. In his haste, he knocked off a box of tissues.

He stretched both legs out on the bed and pointed to his

knees. "I want you to look at these. I wasn't playin' games with you, Ariel."

Fifteen seconds of silence followed. Her hair fell over her shoulders as she looked where he'd directed. He sucked in a breath as she blanketed his swollen knee with a gentle hand, then fingered the scars on the other one.

"I didn't know," she said quietly, looking up. "You didn't tell me how bad—"

"Now you know. The last thing I need is you mad at me, too." He set his feet on the carpet. At the same time he noticed some condoms on the table. "You really did have expectations for tonight."

"Your…last night," she stammered, obviously embarrassed.

He noticed a green nightgown heaped on the floor beside the bed, then remembered she'd been wearing it. She'd replaced it with blue plaid pajamas.

"I can't, Ariel. I hate admitting it, but I just can't."

Her eyes welled up. She set her hands against his face, her thumbs pressed to his mouth. "Shh. Do you think that's what matters most to me? It's all right, Lucas. I'm the one who's sorry. I should have realized how much you were hurting. I did see it at times, then I'd think it was my imagination."

"I know how sensitive you are. I didn't want to be another charity case to you."

She shook her head. A lone tear slid down her cheek. He leaned forward and touched his lips to hers, feeling them quiver.

"Don't make me your project," he said against her mouth. "I'm the man I've always been. No, that's not true. I'm different. But don't treat me differently now, okay?"

"Okay," she whispered. "I just wish you'd told me sooner."

His jaw hardened. "Pride."

"I understand pride. I have too much of it myself."

"Yeah, I know. I admire it, though." He stood. "Good night, Ariel."

"If you need anything—"

"Don't start." He practically growled the words at her.

"Good night," she said meekly.

He grunted, making her laugh. He started to walk away, but he stepped on another condom packet. He make a quick survey to total the packets, then grinned at her. "Four? For one night?"

She turned bright pink.

"You're a demandin' woman, Ariel Minx."

She lifted her chin. "I'm pretty sure you would have risen to the occasion."

Miz Wholesome strikes again. He barked a laugh and walked away, still chuckling as he climbed into his own bed. He could definitely tear up the wife list. He'd found the best woman for the job.

Six

"Don't fuss," Luke said, lifting the plastic bag out of Ariel's reach. "I can manage."

"I just wanted—"

"I know damn well what you wanted to do."

She crossed her arms and leaned against the kitchen counter. The best part of knowing his secret, she decided, was that she got to see him in shorts. His knees were a mess, but the rest of his legs looked pretty darn good.

The timer rang. She opened the oven and pulled out a pan of banana-nut muffins, dumped them into a basket and set them on the table beside the scrambled eggs and sausages she'd plunked down half a minute ago. She watched Luke take a seat and prop up his leg on another chair, the ice pack molded over his knee.

"I thought you already had surgery," she ventured, spearing a sausage. "Didn't it work?"

"On the other knee, which had the most damage at the time. We'd been holding off on this one until I was completely recovered.'' He broke a muffin in two, slathered butter on one half, then popped it in his mouth. ''I reinjured this knee the day before you came up to my office. Can we talk about something else?''

She shoved the sports section of the newspaper his way. ''You might want to check out the editor's Random Notes on the first page.''

''From your tone of voice, I probably don't want to.'' He picked it up anyway and scanned the headline. ''Hell. 'Walker Mystery Solved.'''

''It gets better. Read on.''

'''Speculation on Luke Walker's whereabouts has kept the water cooler and sports-bar conversations at fever pitch all week. Where was the man responsible for last year's big win? Sulking?''' Luke snorted. '''He's been right here in the city, attending to some personal charity work. ''The team made the Super Bowl without me,'' Walker said in a recent interview. ''They don't need any distractions right before the game. And I've been focusing on helping where I'm needed more.'' Charity wouldn't seem to be the only item on his agenda, however. Just who was the blond mystery woman seen dancing cheek-to-cheek with him at a benefit for the Wilson Buckley Youth Center last night? And is he going to support the Dusters today by showing up for the big game? Yes, according to owner Gabe Madison, who says Walker will watch the game from the owner's private box.'''

Luke looked over the top of the paper at Ariel. ''The Center got its plug, anyway. And the reporter doesn't know how right he is when he called you a mystery lady.'' He folded the paper and put it aside. ''You won't be one after today. I can't not introduce you to everyone in the box, Ariel.''

''I thought about that before I accepted your invitation. I figure they'll be too focused on the game to worry about me.''

You haven't met the wives, he thought. *So, what is it that you're hiding, Ariel? And why?*

Ariel might have tried to guess what it meant to be a sports celebrity, but her picture of that life didn't come close to the reality. It started in the parking lot, where a maintenance man spotted Luke and offered them a ride on his cart, snagging himself an autograph in return. Then the walk to the box netted more requests than he could politely handle. She saw him breathe a sigh of relief when they closed the door of the owner's box behind them.

Raw pain settled in his eyes for a moment, but she didn't think the source was his knee. This would be a hard day for him. No matter how much he smiled, no matter how many jokes he told or compliments he brushed aside, the fact was when the game ended today, he wouldn't be their star. Not now, not ever again.

When the stadium announcer welcomed him back over the loudspeakers and almost all of the spectators stood and applauded, he had to lean out of the booth and wave. The television cameras focused tight. Ariel watched the screen inside the owner's box. He was smiling, but he wasn't happy.

As soon as the backslapping afterward stopped, she moved beside him, easing her arm around his waist. After a moment's hesitation, he slid his arm around her shoulder and pulled her close, kissing the top of her head. She felt him shaking. She wished she could wiggle her nose and get them out of there.

Announcing his presence spurred the team somehow, though. They were down by two touchdowns going into the fourth quarter when he waved to the crowd. At the end of the game, the Gold Dusters came out ahead by seven points. The party continued on for an hour, then one by one, the box emptied of guests, leaving just Luke and Ariel.

"If you want to go to the locker room for a while, I understand," she said. "I can just wait here. Gorge myself a little longer on this sumptuous feast."

"No, thanks."

She sat beside him and slipped her hand into his. "Rough day."

"Yeah."

She leaned against his arm and closed her eyes, exhaustion weighing her down. She felt him turn his head her way, then the touch of his lips against her hair.

"Aren't we the pair, darlin'? I think both our candles are burned to the middle, with no room for any more flame."

She yawned. "I could sleep for days."

"Me, too."

"Why don't you stay one more night? You can't fly back home if you're that tired."

"Actually, I've been thinkin'."

"Uh-oh."

"Be nice, now, Ariel. I had a little cabin built recently in the Sierras, near Lake Tahoe. I haven't even spent the night there yet. It's brand-new. I'm just gonna say to hell with everything, and go relax up there for a couple of days. How about comin' with me?"

She pushed back slowly. Their gazes locked. "I've got responsibilities, Lucas."

"So do I. I'm gonna make some calls and delegate. You can, too."

She hesitated.

"You know you want to. How long has it been since you've taken a vacation?"

"Years. Quite literally, years."

"You've earned it. No pressure, Ariel."

She shouldn't. Two whole days with him? She was bound to become even more attracted, *connected,* to him, and she couldn't afford him in her life.

But she wanted this. For herself. For him, even. For the memories that could get her through some dark times. The nightmares hadn't returned the past two nights, after all.

"All right, Lucas. I'll do it."

"What are we sittin' around here for, then? Let's go."

It took hours to clear their calendars and pack their bags. Ariel argued against driving when they were both so tired, but he assured her he was fine and told her just to sleep. She closed her eyes at the first stoplight. That was the last thing she remembered until awakening when the car stopped.

But it wasn't the cabin or a gas station or a restaurant they were parked in front of. It was an airport. A small, private airstrip where he kept his jet.

"Was there something on board you need to take with you?" she asked, her hands closing into fists.

"Thought I'd surprise you." Luke angled her way. "We're gonna fly up. My car's at the airport there. It'll save us—"

"No."

She looked straight ahead, but he didn't think she saw anything.

"You afraid of flyin', Ariel?"

"You should have asked, Lucas. We've just wasted more time. We'll be lucky to make it to your cabin by dawn now."

She sat rigidly, her voice taut and controlled. When he touched her cheek, she jerked away.

"The best way to overcome fear is to face it," he said gently. "Challenge it."

"We're wasting time," she repeated.

"Don't you trust me?"

"I don't trust anyone that much."

"Ariel—"

She faced him. "Don't push. I'm not getting in that plane. There isn't anything—*anything*—you can say to convince me otherwise."

Her eyes were pitch-dark. Her lips were so stiff they barely moved. Still, fear had to be conquered. He'd learned that long ago.

"I've logged hundreds of thousands of miles in planes, a lot of them in that jet right there. It's safer than the drive would be."

She pulled the keys from the ignition. "Get out."

"What the hell? Ariel—be reasonable."

"I'm being perfectly reasonable. It just doesn't match your idea of *reasonable.*"

This was no ordinary fear of flying, he realized. This was terror. No amount of coaxing would change her mind. "I have to cancel the flight plan," he said, eyeing the keys clutched in her hand. "You won't leave me here, will you?"

"No."

Ouch. She was more than a little irritated with him.

"Promise?"

She glared at him in answer. Her predictability factor plummeted a few more notches.

He eased out of the car. As he walked to the terminal, he kept waiting for the sound of her car engine starting up, but it never came. He hurried through his business, then relaxed on the walk back when he saw the car sitting where he'd left it.

"You should've started the engine to keep some heat in here," he said, catching the keys she tossed at him.

"I'm not a child, Lucas. If I'd been cold, I would've done that."

"Anger heats you up, huh?"

Oh, big mistake, he realized, when the air turned frigid. She probably didn't appreciate his sense of humor at the moment.

For the first hour of the drive he tried to talk to her, but she sat with her arms folded, staring out the window, silent.

"Now I'm *really* lookin' forward to two days alone with you," he muttered, his patience gone.

She turned on him like an angry hornet. "Apparently you don't think I know my own mind."

"I have always given you credit for having a mind of your own, Ariel."

"Then why did you treat me like some brainless idiot?"

"I didn't—"

"Doesn't anyone ever say no to you?"

"Plenty of people have said no to me."

"You just don't believe them."

"I don't let it be a permanent road block," he said. "There's a difference."

"The difference being that good ol' Texas charm. I'm immune."

"You're not immune."

She made a violent gesture. "There you go again. Don't tell me how I feel. I know how I feel."

"I can't talk to you when you're like this," he said.

Her jaw dropped. "When I'm like what? I have every reason to be angry."

"I disagree. I was only tryin' to help you conquer your fear."

"Since when are my fears your problem?"

"I guess they're not. Not anymore. Go ahead, Ariel. Let your fear control you. Don't be stronger than it. Why should I care?"

Silence slithered in and stayed, coiled tensely. Eventually he turned on the radio to fill the void.

"And another thing," she said later, as if their conversation had lapsed for only sixty seconds instead of sixty minutes. "If we're going to sleep together, I think we should discuss our sexual histories."

It was Luke's turn to gape. Then he laughed, the sound harsh even to his own ears. "Sleep together? All we've done is fight. Or does arguing put you in the mood?"

"I'll start," she said primly. "Safe sex is important to me. You met Jan. I—"

"It's important to me, too. But at this point, it's a nonissue."

"I can't tolerate the Pill," she continued, "so there's more than one reason for your having to wear protection."

He could see she was determined to deal with this. And she thought *he* was stubborn? Hell. "I've been tested for everything recently because of the surgeries. I'm fine."

"So am I. But I still have to ask you to be in charge of birth control."

"I'm sterile." He clicked off the suddenly loud radio, flooding the car with silence again.

"Lucas."

The whisper of sound hurt deeply. Last night he'd wanted sympathy from her. But not tonight. He'd played the game with other women—pretended to be protecting them from pregnancy by wearing a condom. He hadn't revealed the painful secret before. He hadn't planned on telling Ariel yet. It would just give her another reason to make him her cause. And it was important that she care about him for her own reasons, not because he triggered some altruistic need.

Damn her for backing him into that corner.

"Lucas, I'm so sorry."

"I've dealt with it."

"How long have you known?"

"A long time. Twelve years."

"How did you find out?"

"This isn't a topic I really want to get into with you. You wanted to discuss sexual histories, like the responsible nineties people that we are. We are both apparently disease free. Pregnancy isn't an issue. But frankly, I didn't invite you to the cabin to seduce you. We're both worn out. I thought you could use the time away as much I could."

Ariel looked away from him, wondering if that was true. She'd gotten so many mixed signals from him over their four days together that she didn't know what to believe anymore. When he'd kissed her, when he'd caressed her—that wasn't real? He'd just gotten carried away, as men tend to do so much easier than women? She was just handy?

She welcomed the mental diversion. The longer she could focus on something other than the airplane, the better, although she couldn't avoid it much longer now. He might think he knew how afraid she was, but he couldn't come close to understanding the depth of that fear. The nightmares would return now, probably worse than ever.

No. She wasn't going to worry about it. Not now. For now, she'd think about Luke and the catch in his voice when he'd said he was sterile. Did he think it made him less of a man?

Maybe if she shared something personal with him, they could get back on track.

"I didn't tell you the truth, Lucas," she said, ending the fragile silence. "It isn't that I can't tolerate the Pill, but that I don't have any reason to bother with it. I haven't slept with anyone for years."

He didn't respond for a while, then, "I guess I should be flattered. You had plans last night for me."

"It was presumptuous. I can see that. I had come to some conclusions about your feelings that apparently aren't true. If all you want is rest and relaxation while we're at your cabin, that's fine. I'd just rather know now so that I don't make a fool of myself."

He curved his hand over hers in her lap. "Your voice is shaky. You've gotten teary-eyed a whole bunch of times lately. It doesn't take a genius to figure out that you're strung tight. You've been runnin' on steam since I got to your place, and somehow I don't think it's anything new to you. I'm worried about you."

"And that's why you invited me to spend two days alone with you in a deserted mountain cabin, where we might even get snowed in?" She looked around her. They weren't more than fifteen minutes away from Lake Tahoe. A quiet drift of snow had been falling for the past few miles. "Knowing I'm attracted to you, you invited me? That borders on sadistic, Lucas."

"I never intended to hurt you."

"And you also never intended to sleep with me, right?"

"Don't put words in my mouth."

"The answer is, 'No, Ariel, I don't want to sleep with you.' Just say it."

"You're a beautiful, desirable woman—"

"Just say it, Lucas."

"I can't."

"Because it isn't true, or because you don't want to hurt my feelings? Because I'm fine with whatever the reason is."

"Let's just take this time together and see what happens, Ariel. How's that for an answer?"

"I can live with that."

She looked at him just in time to see him nod.

"And this is the master bedroom," Luke said.

Ariel followed him into the last room on his brief, guided tour. The small but luxurious cabin definitely had Luke's stamp on it. As in his office, the furnishings were chosen for comfort, not to impress, although they were distinctly masculine. The master bedroom boasted a huge bed with an inviting sapphire blue comforter, simple pine furnishings and a hot tub nestled within a glassed-in niche. The view of the majestic forest beyond was imposing. The sun was just beginning to light up the day. Fresh snow glistened on the trees and the rocks, turning the sight into a picture postcard as more flakes drifted steadily down.

Luke yawned and stretched. "I'm gonna catch a few hours' sleep. How about you?"

Ariel feared sleep, and the nightmares sure to follow. She had to delay them as long as possible. "I'm too keyed up for now. I'll check out the groceries someone so nicely delivered in the middle of the night. I still can't believe you can make a phone call and have that sort of thing taken care of. Heat turned on, road plowed."

"Celebrity has to have its privileges, darlin', to balance the sacrifices. Plus my caretaker is well compensated for his trouble." He combed her hair from her face, then touched a finger to her chin, lifting it. "You're welcome to use the hot tub, if you want. Might help you sleep."

"With you sleeping in the same room?"

"If that makes you uncomfortable, there's a smaller whirlpool tub in the guest bathroom. You just don't have a view from there."

She watched him unbutton the flannel shirt he wore. "I might do that. You're not concerned about someone seeing in here? I noticed there aren't any curtains."

"Those little bars at the ceiling have blinds I can lower. But this place is so remote, I don't really worry about it. As I said, I haven't spent the night here before. Maybe I'll feel differently when it's dark outside." He shrugged out of his shirt, grabbed the long-sleeved, thermal shirt beneath it at the waist, then pulled it over his head.

Ariel stared at his chest. She didn't want to. She just couldn't help it. "Um, Lucas?"

He sat on the bed and untied his boots. "What?"

"How's your knee?"

"Killin' me. Why?" One boot fell to the floor.

"Just wondering."

The other boot dropped. His socks followed. She didn't move. Just his jeans left. He stood. His long fingers touched the top button. "You plannin' on tuckin' me in bed, darlin'?"

"No." She looked at his face, caught his one-sided smile. "I, um, I thought you might want an ice pack."

"I'd appreciate that."

She scooted out of the room faster than he could say thank you. Luke chuckled to himself. A few women had watched him undress before, but not one of them had looked at him like Ariel just had. There was that fake look women sometimes used, like you were a Greek god or something, and they couldn't wait to get their hands on you, when actually all they wanted was for you to perform for them, be some kind of perfect stud, the likes of which was never before known to mankind. Did they really think being famous meant a man was better in the sack? Did they really think he wouldn't appreciate a woman taking the lead once in a while and pleasuring him, as well?

Women. They were complex creatures.

Then there was Ariel. The most complex of all.

He didn't believe she played the same kind of games. In fact, he was glad she'd lost her temper with him. At least it was honest.

He left his shorts on and slipped under the covers just as she came back into the room, an ice pack in hand.

"You took your pill?" she asked.

"Yes, Mom."

She hefted the bag of ice, contemplating it.

"My knee, please, darlin'."

She moved to the side of the bed. With a wicked smile, she dropped it in his lap.

Although cushioned by the comforter, it still shocked him. "Why you—"

"Don't mess with me, Walker. I get even."

He adjusted the comforter so that he could stick out his leg, shoved a pillow under his knee, then settled the pack. "I'll remember that. Are you really not gonna try to sleep?"

"I don't know. Why?"

"If you're still awake in twenty minutes, could you make sure the pack is off my knee? I'm not supposed to let it go beyond that."

"Sure."

"Thanks."

He watched her walk out of the room, then he tucked his hands behind his head. For as tired as he was, his mind didn't want to slow down. He closed his eyes, but sleep eluded him. Just about the time he was going to get rid of the ice, he heard her come into the room.

Without letting himself wonder why, he pretended to be asleep. Her perfume drifted over him. From behind his lids her shadow alerted him she'd come close. He felt the pack be lifted away, then her warm hand molded his cold flesh for a few seconds. A faint sigh came from her as she crouched beside him. He held himself still as her fingers drifted lightly up his thigh, as if she couldn't help herself, before she pulled the comforter over his leg.

Pain free for the first time in hours, he let himself enjoy the surprising moment. Her fingertips grazed his chest hair, like feathers dusting delicate crystal. He hid his reaction by making a sleepy kind of movement, then settling again. Beneath the comforter, his body reacted to her presence, to her scent, to her touch, as she pulled the quilt over his shoulders. Aroused now, he debated whether to pretend to just wake up.

She pressed her lips to his forehead, the gentlest of touches, then she left.

How was it possible that she could arouse him and comfort him in the same moment? Was that the unique skill of an earth angel?

No answer got past the buzz of impending sleep droning in his head.

Seven

Luke glanced at the mantel clock, then out the living room window again. Eleven o'clock. Where was she? He'd awakened twenty minutes ago, showered and shaved, then discovered she wasn't in the cabin. Her car keys lay on the mantel where he'd left them. Which meant she had gone for a walk. In the snow. In unfamiliar territory.

He watched the flakes fall, heavier now than when he'd gone to sleep. Drifts were piling high around the tree bases, although not quite knee-high in the open areas. The main road was half a mile away. The snow was falling so thickly that he couldn't see beyond twenty feet. He squinted, desperate for any sign of her, muttering just about every swear word he knew.

He'd bought the property for the very isolation he now cursed. He didn't dare try to track her. Not knowing which direction she might have gone, plus knowing his knee couldn't tolerate a hike of any distance through snow, he was left to wait—and worry.

She's a grown woman. She wouldn't wander far afield, he reminded himself.

He pounded the window frame with his fist. Why hadn't she just taken a nap? What haunted her so much that she couldn't sleep?

Why hadn't he just tumbled her into bed with him and made love to her, keeping her close?

He wiped a hand down his face, frustrated. He'd done his damnedest not to have lust dominate this relationship like others in the past. And his efforts had paid off, too. By keeping his hands off her most of the time, they were getting to know each other, like each other, admire each other. He'd never had a soul mate. Hadn't really believed such a thing existed.

He was beginning to believe she was his.

As for sex, he'd relegated it to the bottom of his list of needs. It kept trying to creep higher, but so far he was winning the battle it waged to regain its old place of importance in his life. It helped, of course, that his aching knee demanded so much attention.

He saw movement out of the corner of his eye, a splash of red against the white backdrop, moving toward the cabin. Relieved, he shut his eyes for a few seconds.

When she stomped her boots on the porch to dislodge the snow, he opened the front door, intending to chew her out for not leaving him a note.

"You're awake!" she said with a brilliant smile, as if nothing in the world could have made her happier.

He stuck his hands in his pockets. "Have a nice walk?"

She shivered dramatically. "Bone-chilling cold and so quiet you'd think you weren't on earth. Just a bird singing every now and then, or the sound of snow falling in clumps off a tree limb. It's glorious, Lucas. You've created your own heaven."

As she started to step past him in the doorway, he stopped her by gripping her upper arms.

"What's wrong?"

He tugged her into his arms and held her. Just held her. It's what a husband would do, right? He needed to focus on husband kind of stuff for these couple of days. Let her get used to having him do things for her, like warming her up or keeping her safe. Let himself accept the little things she did for him, like reminding him to take his medication. Like sleeping with—

Hell. He wasn't doing a very good job at keeping sex out of his thoughts. He pulled her closer, her down jacket mashed between them.

Gradually the cold seeped from her to him. He shoved the front door shut and rested against it, taking pressure off his leg. After he slid a hand around to snag her zipper and pull it down, her jacket fell off her shoulders and down her arms, landing with a quiet whoosh. He tucked her head under his chin and wrapped her in his arms again. The softest of sighs came from her as she nestled there, giving warmth back, creating a whole new heat at the same time.

Her knit hat drifted to the floor as he dove his fingers through her hair, then cupped the back of her head, holding her still against him. Her arms tightened around him. Their contact wasn't extraordinarily intimate, yet fire spread and raged.

He released her out of necessity. The bedroom seemed so close, so temptingly close. "Don't wander off by yourself again, please."

She looked quizzically at him. "There was no danger."

"You don't know the area. And snow is disorienting."

"I kept the cabin in sight. When the snow got too thick, I headed back." She picked up her jacket, peeled off her mittens and tucked them in the pockets. "I'm not used to having someone worry about me."

"Probably ticks you off, huh?"

She made a "maybe" movement with her head. "I know I'm too defensive."

"And stubborn," he said. Before she could fire back, he

threw his arm around her shoulder and pulled her along with him to the kitchen. "I'll fix you breakfast."

The day passed. They ate when they felt like it, drank copious amounts of hot chocolate and played Monopoly by the fire. But as much as he tried to keep things easy between them, her steadily increasing exhaustion took its toll. She argued about everything, as if she had no control over her words. Irrationality wasn't what he'd come to expect from her.

He shuffled a deck of cards for a fifth game of gin rummy as she poked at the fire. His gaze settled on her tempting behind as she leaned over the fireplace. He forced himself to look at the clock instead. "Would you rather just go to bed?" he asked, seeing that it was past nine.

"If I want to go to bed, I'll just go," she snapped.

He watched her shoulders droop. She regretted her words. She would apologize any second now.

"I'm sorry," she said, sitting on the floor near him again, a sofa cushion at her back. "I don't know what's gotten into me."

He tried to be sympathetic, which wasn't easy when he knew she was creating her own problems. They hadn't talked about her reasons for not getting into his plane last night. At some point they needed to. For her to lose so much sleep over it gave it even greater importance.

And it could be an issue later. A big issue. Maybe an insurmountable one.

He had to get her on board once, that's all. That'd change her mind. Nothing matched his jet for smooth and comfortable flying.

"You're just tired," he said, more patient than he could ever remember being with anyone. "Or maybe it's that time of month?"

Ariel picked up her cards and sorted them. "Had a lot of experience with PMS, Lucas?"

"Enough, I s'pose."

"So, how many women have you slept with?"

He eyed her discard, then chose a card from the deck. "I haven't kept a tally, darlin'. No little black book with ratings in it, either."

"You've been in love, though."

"I guess."

She looked up. "You've been engaged twice."

"I was young."

"How young?"

"You gonna discard?"

She plucked a card and tossed it down. "How young?"

"Nineteen the first time. Twenty-two the second."

"And you didn't love either of them?"

"Now, I didn't say that. I thought I did at the time. How about you? You ever been engaged or married? Had any kids I don't know about?"

"If I had a child, you'd know, Lucas. I also told you I have no plans to marry."

"That doesn't mean you haven't been married." He looked at her. "Or engaged."

"Neither." She picked up ten cards, all the way back to the first card she'd discarded, then used five of them to lay down two runs.

"Hey, I needed that queen," he said.

"Then you should've picked it up."

"It's called strategy. I was bidin' my time."

"Well, you bided too long. So, tell me about your former fiancées."

"Nope."

"Why not?"

"'Cause a gentleman doesn't kiss and tell."

"I'm not asking for sexual details, Lucas. What were they like? Why did the engagements end?"

"I hardly remember either of 'em. Why don't you discard something I can use?"

"Who broke the engagements, you or them?"

"You're a nosy little thing."

"Curious. There's a difference." She hesitated, debating

how much to push. "You said you found out twelve years ago that you were sterile, and twelve years ago you were engaged to your second fiancée. Was that a problem for her, Lucas? She couldn't accept that?"

Luke discarded, the action precise and controlled. "Could you?"

"Of course I could. Are you saying that she couldn't?"

"You know, Ariel, I can't for the life of me figure out why you think it's any concern of yours. If we were engaged or something, then maybe you'd have a right to ask. And maybe I would give you answers. But for now I'll keep my own confidences, the same as you keep yours."

She'd been waiting for this. "If you're referring to last night—"

"Here's the difference. What happened last night *is* between us. It's not in the past. It doesn't involve anyone else. And it's important, because I fly a lot. I like to fly. The FAA would have to ground me before I'd give it up. So, yes, what happened last night matters. You don't owe me an explanation, but I would appreciate one."

She drew a card and studied it, shifted a few cards around, then laid them all down. "Gin. You shouldn't have held on to those aces, Lucas. I just caught up to you."

"Well, shoot." He tallied the points and marked them on the score pad. "So much for strategy."

Luke watched her yawn and stretch, showing no intention of explaining about last night and every intention of avoiding the subject altogether. "Going to bed?"

She nodded. "Can I fix your ice pack?" she asked.

"I can do it."

They stood together. Luke cupped her cheek, and she looked up at him. "I wish you'd let me help," he said. "I'm a good listener."

Her eyes took on some sparkle. "Is that so?"

"It's a skill I use sparingly, mind you. Wouldn't want to get a reputation for bein' one of those sensitive kinda males women talk about wantin' today. Saps." He trailed his thumb across her lips as she started to laugh, watched as they parted, moist and enticing.

She grabbed his hand with both of hers, pulled it to rest against her heart, the sweater she wore cushioning more than it teased. "Make up your mind, Lucas."

"About what?"

"I can't walk this tightrope. You can't seem to decide whether to kiss me or not. Whether to make love with me or not."

"It's not a matter of whether. It's a matter of tryin' to do the right thing. I don't want to take advantage," he said. "You're so tired you can hardly keep your eyes open, yet you seem afraid to shut them. I didn't mean to, but somehow I caused you trauma last night."

"This has been a tough time for you, as well. But we're adults and healthy. Relatively healthy, anyway. I guess because of your knee, I'd have to be on top."

Luke fought reacting. The image came, stark and erotic, of Ariel riding him, her hair sliding around her shoulders, her breasts filling his hands. She always moaned when they kissed. Imagine when they made love—

Dangerous thoughts, these. And if she hadn't grinned like a mischievous five-year-old just then, he might have done some experimenting. But she'd said the words to prove a point—that women held all the power. It wasn't really a surprise to him, but the reminder served him well.

And pretty much ticked him off.

He hauled her to him and kissed her. Kissed her mischievous mouth and felt her smile soften after a second, her lips going slack, then molding to his as she rose on tiptoe and fitted herself to his body. She moaned. She messed up his hair as she dove her fingers through it, tugging herself closer. He kissed her harder, deeper, longer. His body made a liar of him—the punishment was his, not hers. He ached for her.

Because of it, he moved her back. "Does that answer one of your concerns, darlin'?"

Her sleepy, dreamy smile teased him as she angled closer,

laying a hand on his chest. She dragged her palm down his stomach and beyond, until she covered his hardness. "And this answers another one. Can you resist for yet another day, Lucas?"

She didn't wait for his answer. She said good-night and walked away. He seriously considered using the ice pack he was about to make on a completely different part of his body.

A few minutes later he settled into bed, his knee propped on a pillow. He'd heard the whirlpool come on in the guest bathroom. To help her sleep or to continue to help her not sleep? he wondered. He lay there for the prescribed twenty minutes, then got up to dump the ice. From inside his bathroom he could hear the whirlpool still going in the room next door. She'd be a prune if she stayed in there much longer.

He sat on his bed another five minutes, listening, waiting. Still the motor ran. What if she'd fallen asleep?

After slipping into his bathrobe, he opened his door and padded across the carpet to listen at hers. The motor droned. He looked at the floor, debating. Did he have a right to enter? Would she be furious at him for checking up on her?

Deciding the risk was worth it, he knocked. No answer. He called her name. No reply. Carefully, he turned the knob and eased open the door. A bedside light was on. She wasn't in bed.

He called her name again from just outside the bathroom. When she didn't respond, he tapped the door with his fingertips, setting it in motion. With a quiet thud, it hit the wall.

The room was well lit. The bath water bubbled and bubbled, then stopped, bringing a silence that sounded louder than the noise. The timer must have shut off.

Ariel wasn't in the tub.

He hurried out of the suite, down the hall, and into the living room, lit only by the dying fire. No sign of her.

He moved into the kitchen. Empty.

He stood in the middle of the room and turned a full circle, running his hands through his hair. Where the hell was she? Were her car keys still on the mantel?

While returning to the living room he saw that the front door was unlocked. He'd checked it right before bed. It was locked.

She couldn't be—

He opened the front door and saw her standing on the porch, hugging herself, her hair dusted white, her feet covered with fresh snow. Her robe wasn't a thick, cuddly fabric designed to ward off the cold, but a silky wrap.

"Ariel." He said her name quietly, so as not to startle her. The snow stung his feet as he walked to her. "What are you doing out here?"

"T-trying t-to stay aw-wake."

"Why?" He didn't know whether to touch her. She was brittle with tension. He didn't want to make it worse.

"B-bec-cause I-I don't w-want to s-see it any-anymore."

"See what, angel?"

She spun around and faced him, her eyes wide. "W-what d-did you c-call me? W-what?"

"Angel."

"W-why?"

"Can we go inside? You're going to freeze." His calmness was an act, but she couldn't know it. Someone had to stay in control. The task had fallen to him.

"I'll f-fall asleep. I c-can't fall as-sleep."

"I'll help you stay awake." He wrapped a hand around her elbow to guide her. She stumbled once, then went with him into the house. He wished he could carry her. He couldn't. His knee would buckle.

"Sit on the couch. I'll get the fire going again."

She sat where he put her, accepted the blanket he wrapped around her. Her teeth chattered.

He'd never seen anything like it. Oh, he knew she lived with some kind of demon, but this was beyond anything he could have imagined. As soon as the fire took hold, he sat beside her and drew her legs into his lap. He shoved his robe aside and settled her feet against his stomach, trying not to show any reaction to her icy skin pressing against him.

"Talk to me, Ariel. It's not going to go away this time. Even I can see that. Trust me. Tell me about your nightmare. This has something to do with flying, doesn't it?"

"Yes."

He waited through her silence. "I don't want to guess wrong. Tell me."

"Why did you call me a-angel?"

He moved her feet to warmer places along his sides, kept his hands curved over the tops of her feet. "I've always thought of you that way. An earth angel."

She looked away. "My family called me that."

"You told me your aunt raised you. What happened to your family?"

"They died." Her voice caught. "They all died."

God, no. He struggled to find his voice, to keep her talking, to free her from the nightmare. "In a plane?"

She nodded. She tugged the blanket higher around her and focused on some spot beyond him. "The weather was horrible." She closed her eyes and shuddered. "Wind shears, they said, after. The plane slammed straight into a mountain and broke apart. Rows of seats from the tail section were ejected. Fire got the rest of the plane—and the people. My mom and dad, my little brother, my grandparents. All gone."

The lack of inflection in her voice frightened him. He wanted her to get angry. To cry. To scream. To fight the memory. "I'm sorry," he said softly, hoping his sympathy would draw some emotion. "Ariel, I'm so sorry."

She looked at him then, seemed to realize who he was, where she was. "No one should die like that, Lucas."

A hot ache consumed him. "No."

"I was only eight years old, and in sixty seconds I lost everyone who mattered to me. Everyone."

"Why weren't you with them?"

"I was," she whispered. "I was there."

He breathed her name. No.

Tremors overtook her, first her hands, then her arms, then

the quaking worked its way down her body. Her words came out broken and raspy and terrifyingly vivid.

"I remember the light—the lightning. I remember the plane sputtering. Sputtering. Sputtering. Losing altitude. And the sc-screams. God, the—the screams. All around me. All around me. Mine, mostly. Then the fire and the smoke and horror. I couldn't m-move. I tried to call to my mom— Oh, God, my mom! But I couldn't get a sound out."

Luke shifted so that he could hold her. He was afraid she would fight it, but she went limp in his arms except for an occasional shudder of leftover emotion. He wished she would cry.

"The next thing I remember clearly was a man lifting me in his arms. 'I've got you,' he said. 'I've got you.' He just kept saying it, as if he didn't believe it, either. He was big and kind and gentle, and I just curled up in his arms like a baby. He had a beard. It was wet from the rain. He took off his jacket and put it around me. I got lost in it. Lost... Oh, I was so lost."

He stroked her hair, again and again. "Was he another passenger?"

She shook her head. "A rescuer."

"How long after the crash?"

"Hours. We landed in a forest, it was night, and there was the rain, too."

"Were you conscious?"

"Off and on. I haven't been on a plane since. I never intend to." She let out a ragged breath. "I don't want to talk about it anymore."

"What can I do for you, Ariel? How can I help?"

"I don't want to be alone tonight."

He buried his face in her hair, still damp with melting snow. "You don't have to be alone. Do you want some hot tea?"

"Just your arms. Please. Just your arms. Don't leave me, Lucas."

"I won't leave you. Let's go to bed."

Eight

Somewhere between the living room and the bedroom Ariel locked up her nightmare again. She'd become an expert at keeping it out of her conscious mind. The dreams should end now that she'd told him. She was safe again. For the moment.

When they reached the bed, he lifted the covers and she slid under them. He turned off the light. She could hear his robe fall to the carpet, then he was beside her, drawing her near. She felt his caution as he eased up next to her so that he could hold her. She nestled against him instantly, found the perfect place to burrow, her nose pressed to his neck, just below his ear. His scent comforted her in a way that nothing else could, familiar and cherished, making her feel safe.

She closed her eyes, hoping for sleep, but was so aware of him she thought she would never sleep again. Minutes ticked by, but life came to a stop. There was no world but theirs, no pain but hers, no comfort but his.

"I'm glad you told me," he said into the darkness.

"I didn't seem to have much choice." She inched closer. Her foot touched his. "I guess I should've told you sooner." She tipped her head back, seeking him in the dark, pulling herself a little closer with the movement. "Thank you for finding me. I'm not sure how long I would have stayed out—"

"Shh."

She shoved the memories aside with an efficiency born of years of practice. She tried again to sleep. But her hands wouldn't stay still. She needed to touch him, to know he was there, to know he wasn't going to leave her, not even to turn to his other side.

"Lucas," she whispered.

"What, darlin'?"

Her eyes burned at the tenderness in his voice. "Nothing."

"Tell me."

"I just wanted to say your name. I like your name. Have I told you that?"

"No."

"Well, I do. I know I'm snippy with you sometimes. I don't mean to be."

"I like when you're snippy."

"Really?"

"Yeah."

"Why?"

"I don't know. I just do. Ariel?"

"What?"

"Close your eyes, darlin'. Try to sleep. I promise I'm not going to leave you for a second."

"I'm sorry."

"For what?"

"For being so needy."

He seemed to give up on keeping any distance between them, for he suddenly pulled her snug against him. Their legs intertwined. Her breasts brushed his chest, then flattened against him. She felt his hand stroke her hair, then drift lower, down her back, over her rear, the silk of her robe warming with each stroke. He repeated the motion again and again. He probably meant to soothe. The effect was far from soothing.

Her nipples drew taut. She wriggled downward, until she could press her lips to his collarbone. Her fingers combed the surprisingly soft hair that spread across his chest, tapering to just one tempting line, a line she followed with her finger until she reached a fabric barrier. She danced her fingers back up the path, then toyed with some strands, finding an odd sort of comfort in the action.

"I do need you, Lucas."

He said her name, low and harsh. Tipping her head back, she waited.

He leaned down to her, until he could touch his lips to hers. His tongue sought entry and she gave it willingly. Such tenderness, such care, he offered.

The gentle kiss went on and on, for minutes, for an hour, it seemed. Only their lips touched with intimacy. She squirmed finally, anxious for more. Maybe he was just appeasing her. Maybe—

She pulled back. "I don't want sympathy sex, Lucas."

Luke captured her hand and pushed it down his body until she could gauge his involvement in the moment. "Sympathy?"

"Men get interested easier—"

"I'm not feeling the least sympathetic, Ariel. And I don't hear a clock ticking, either. Do you?"

"What do you mean?"

"What's your hurry?" He wanted to drag it out, to drive her crazy, to make her put everything behind her but what she could feel right then. Ariel was the important one here. Only Ariel. "Just enjoy it."

She made that soft little moan he loved when he slid a hand under her robe and cupped her breast. The sound deepened when he brushed his thumb across her nipple. He raised up on an elbow, then toyed with the sash of her robe until it fell away, the slippery fabric sliding down her arms easily as she rolled from one side to the other to free herself of the garment. He pushed his shorts off and shoved them to the bottom of the bed with his foot.

Then they were flesh to flesh, warm and anxious and thoroughly aroused. He kissed her, a leisurely caress that intensified second by second, breath by breath. He left a damp trail down her throat as he ventured lower, until he found the peak of her breast and stroked it with his tongue until it stiffened impossibly.

He heard her suck in a deep breath as he closed his mouth over the hard round peak. She tasted good, smelled good. She moved, arched, sighed, rocked. Every part of her responded to the moment.

An uncharacteristic need to be in command tied him up, not within a silky web but as if with ropes, taut and unyielding. She would want equality. He didn't want to give it to her. She would want to give as much pleasure as she received. He wanted to see how many times he could pleasure her.

He covered her body with his, settled his legs between hers. "Be still," he said softly, weaving his fingers with hers, sliding her arms straight out, imprisoning her. He wanted to feel her quiver. He wanted to hear her pant, trying to hold back her response. "Just lie there."

"Lucas." She groaned his name, lifted her hips higher.

"Shh." He let more of his weight rest on her.

She went still. Their bodies touched all the way down. He didn't attempt to join with her. He had to control it, make it right for her. The pleasure had to be hers. All hers.

He kissed her. He hadn't cared this much about kissing before, but he'd never had a woman need him so much, either. It wasn't his imagination. She told him so in husky little whispers and breathy little sighs.

"I need to hold you," she panted. "Let go so I can."

"No."

"Lucas." She tugged, trying to pull her hands from his.

He tightened his grip. He had all the control. He liked it. He liked it way too much. "Just feel, Ariel. Just feel."

"I'm feeling." She dragged the word out, the tone deepening as he entered her just a little. "Oh, you feel good. So good."

It was all the encouragement he needed to go even more slowly, to feel her wrap velvet around him, quarter inch by quarter inch, to feel her squeeze him from within, to feel the waves of her climax, one after another after another as he filled her.

He finally released her so that he could cradle her rear with both hands, bringing her up tightly to him again, putting pressure where it would take her higher. Again he felt her squeeze him rhythmically from within. Again she cried out.

He ducked his head and drew a hard nipple into his mouth at the moment she peaked. He fought the mind-shocking power of her reaction as she wrapped her legs around him higher, but it was stronger than he was. Hard, rhythmic thrusts. Coiled heat. A lethal mix of her long, low moan and her teeth sinking into his shoulder, then he joined her in the pleasure, the explosion of light and sound and motion a far cry from the gentleness he'd planned to distract her, soothe her, comfort her. A far cry from anything in his experience. Or even his fantasies.

She melted beneath him, although her arms stayed draped around him, keeping him where he lay. He absorbed the experience, waited for the pleasure to wane and the surprise to settle. Earth shattering. He finally knew what the term meant.

"I've got to move," he said apologetically. "My knee..."

No answer.

"Ariel?" He drew back.

She was sound asleep.

Asleep, hell. She was practically unconscious. Well, he'd never had that effect on a woman before. So much for gentle and considerate. He was so considerate, he'd put her to sleep. He smiled at the thought. He'd satisfied her, though, even if it hadn't gone exactly to his plan.

Careful not to jar her too much, he moved off her, then tucked her close again. She nestled instinctively, made a soft little sound of contentment, then went all loose limbed. He ran his fingers lightly through her hair. Where would they go from here? They had a full day ahead of them, and while he wouldn't mind too much spending the time in bed, she needed something else right now—consideration for her tender emotional state.

He couldn't give in to the need he already had for her again. She deserved better than that. This relationship wasn't going to perish because passion ruled it, like the others had.

Respect, admiration, friendship. Those were his goals. He'd get her to open up by sharing his—he shuddered—feelings. Then by the time they ended their vacation, she'd be willing to listen to reason about marriage.

She'd probably fight it at first. But he'd win. She needed him. All he had to do was to make her see that.

Clouds. She dreamed of clouds and peace and joy. And blue sky as far as the eye could see. And sunshine. And warmth.

Warmth. She snuggled into it, absorbed it like a prisoner coming out of solitary confinement. Her mind was a blank, except for a sense of well-being.

She opened her eyes. She was wrapped in Luke's arms, as she must have been all night long. She lifted her head to look at the clock.

"Almost ten," he said drowsily, rubbing her back as she stretched against him. "You slept hard."

"And without dreams, thanks to you." She relaxed, not willing to end the moment. His scent was so familiar now. So dear. His morning voice rumbled comfortingly from his chest. She wove her fingers through the mat of hair, swirled around his nipple, teased it when it hardened.

"Uh, darlin'?"

"Hmm?"

"I kinda need to get up."

"My plan exactly."

He chuckled. "I mean, I need to get out of bed. I hate to sound like a broken record, but I'm way past takin' something for my knee, and it's killin' me."

Disappointed, she sat up, giving him room. The room was chilly, but she let the comforter fall behind her. She liked that he focused on her breasts. She would have worried if he hadn't. He hadn't seemed as involved last night as she was. "Are you sure I can't delay you for just a few minutes?"

"Just a few minutes? Why, darlin', that's not a problem I seem to have. Has it been your past experience?" He flung the comforter aside as he climbed out of bed. At some point during the night, he'd put his shorts on.

Ariel watched him scoop up his robe and head toward the door. "Not last night," she said, earning a cocky smile before he left.

"Definitely not last night," she repeated to herself as she dragged the quilt up and snuggled into it. Last night he'd made love to her with all-consuming attention, yet it almost seemed planned. As if he hadn't intended to get anything out of it for himself.

She'd never been kissed so well, leaving her feeling almost drugged just from the way he used his mouth to arouse her, as if he was determined not to touch her otherwise. Of course, he had, eventually. And it had been wonderful, even though he hadn't given her a chance to return the exploration. He'd held her arms straight out beside her, and then the moment he'd eased into her, filling her so completely and beautifully, she'd climaxed. The instant they joined. Imagine.

She sighed. Was it because it had been such a long time for her?

No. It was Luke. That's all. Just because he'd apparently had a lot of practice—

She frowned, not liking the unfamiliar and unwanted twinge of jealousy that tapped her on the shoulder and said hello.

When he didn't return after a few minutes, she headed for the bathroom, washed up a little, then searched him out, tying on her robe as she went. She found him on the sofa with his leg propped up and his eyes closed.

"You're in a lot of pain," she said, tamping down the hurt that he hadn't come back to the bedroom but had remained out here by himself.

"Yeah."

She sat on the coffee table, her knees level with his waist. He'd started the fire, and it blazed behind her now, warming the room. She felt cold, anyway. "What's the next course of action?"

"Surgery."

"When?"

"Soon."

His one-word responses eroded her self-confidence completely. She lifted the ice pack and appraised his knee. "Looks really bad today."

"Yeah."

"You should've let me be on top."

Luke opened his eyes. She rested her forearms on her thighs, clasped her hands and smiled, although tentatively. His gaze drifted down the vee of fabric. He focused on the creamy skin revealed by her partially open robe. He couldn't see her nipples, but the way she sat pressed her breasts together. He had a nice view. An intentionally nice view. "I didn't hear any complaints last night."

"I didn't have any." She rubbed her hands together, the movement stiff. "What's wrong, Lucas?"

"Wrong?"

"Am I way off base or are you regretting last night?"

"No regrets at all."

"Then why have you been running from me since we woke up? *Was* that just sympathy sex last night?"

Stalling, he tugged her robe together, blocking his view of temptation.

"It's worse than I thought," she said, a look of horror

crossing her face. "You felt sorry for me. Oh, God. How could you do that? How could you?" She pushed herself to standing, folded her arms over her stomach. "I'm going to take a shower, then I'll leave. I'm sure someone will come get you when you're ready."

"Don't go." He caught the hem of her robe as she turned away. "You're putting words in my mouth. Sit down. Please."

She didn't move, but she didn't sit, either. He almost smiled. Stubborn woman. The plan he'd concocted last night in the mellow aftermath of lovemaking seemed useless now. When she was asleep in his arms, he'd thought he had all the answers. Talk, share, learn. It still was a noble plan, if slightly impossible. She was not easily diverted from a goal, that goal being a few more rounds of lovemaking, he suspected. He was trying his hardest to block that image.

"Last night was not a mistake," he said. "It had been building for days. Technically, it'd been building since the last night on the cruise ship last June. It's just that I've had too many relationships fall apart once things got physical. My fault entirely, mind you. I don't want that to happen with you."

She sat on the table again. "So, you have a short attention span once sex is involved? We live over two hundred miles apart, Lucas. We won't see each other daily, or even weekly. You're the first man I've both trusted and liked enough to be intimate with in a long, long time. I thought you wanted the same thing."

"I don't think we do want the same things, Ariel." He captured her hand as she straightened, obviously hurt. "Football has been the biggest part of my life since I was ten. That's twenty-four years. How do I shut the door on that life and start fresh? That's what I'm trying to figure out. You know who you are. I envy that."

Ariel knew all about shutting doors and starting fresh. Sympathetic to a fellow seeker, she squeezed his hand. "Tell me about your life."

He relaxed into the cushions. "I was born and raised in northeast Texas. My parents still live there."

"Any siblings?"

"Nope. Just Mom and Dad. He's a sculptor, if you can believe it. She's a poet. Published quite a few books."

She smiled. "I can't picture it. That is, I can't picture you coming from them."

"Dad's a great big guy, taller than me, heavier, but probably the gentlest man on God's green earth. Mom's tall, too, and as skinny as Olive Oyl. They have this—" he struggled for the right word "—connection between them. They communicate with looks and gestures more than with words, like their souls are cosmically joined. I always felt the odd man out. For a long time I thought that I must have been adopted. It's why I focused so much on football. I had a sense of family all the time from my team. I knew my place there."

"Were you always a star?"

He shrugged. "I've always had the gift of gab, which makes for easy media contact. I wasn't radically controversial. There was the party boy image that the public seemed to eat up, but I've been careful to keep my nose clean. That's not to say I didn't shut down my share of bars in my time, especially the first few years. Mostly I just worked harder than the average. I don't know if I had more talent, but I was willing to pay the price to stay in the game."

"The price being your knees?"

"That's part of it. I achieved a lot of recognition from early on. The pressure is unbelievable. I was lucky to have an off-season job—and a grandfather who doesn't take crap from anyone—to keep me in line. If anyone's my role model, it's Granddad. Hardest-working man I know. Eighty-two years old and still the CEO. Still at work every day, at least until this trip around the country."

"You said you'd worked for Titan for a long time."

"Ever since I graduated and turned pro. My grandparents—my mother's parents—started the business on a shoestring, they like to say. The company has built steadily through the years. When I graduated from college, Granddad offered me a job during the off season. I started in the mail room and worked my way up, held almost every position there at one time or another, although PR was my specialty. My degree's in business, and I've been around since the birth of the athletic-shoe industry as big business, so I understood the potential of Titan beyond anything Granddad imagined. And now that's he's turned it over to me, I'm plannin' to go play with the big boys."

"I don't think he just turned it over. You must have earned it."

He shrugged. "I was offered a front office job with the Dusters. And a couple of television networks wanted me to audition for a broadcasting position. But I wanted to have a normal life. It's hard enough walking away from the game. To stay that involved peripherally would just delay the inevitable."

The challenge he'd presented himself would help him find the person, the life, he was searching for, Ariel knew. He didn't need her help in figuring out how to shut the door on his past. He was already doing it.

He lifted the ice pack off, set it on the floor beside him and swung his legs around to sit up. He took both her hands in his.

"Do you want to talk about your family? Because I'd be glad to listen."

"I wish I had more memories of them. My aunt made me talk about them incessantly at the beginning, until I had a book about them in my head. I can open it to the pages I want or need anytime. I am the historian, my aunt says. The story keeper. Sometime I'll tell you. Everything's a little raw right now." She leaned forward and pressed her lips to his. "Thank you for last night. It meant a lot."

"My pleasure."

She cupped his cheek. "Not only in bed. You were...careful with me. You didn't push. I know you must have a lot of questions. I'm just not up to answering them."

And his questions would lead to more revelations she just wasn't ready to make. She plucked at her robe. "I need a shower. I'll fix us omelets afterward, okay?"

Ariel used the shower in the master bedroom, telling herself there was no sense in their using both showers, but hoping that Luke would join her. After a few minutes, she realized he wasn't going to. She tried to put it out of her mind.

The hot water soothed her, helped her not to think about him and the fact he didn't want to sleep with her again. She didn't understand it. They were single, uncommitted elsewhere and healthy. Pregnancy wasn't a fear. So what stopped him? She wanted a physical relationship with him. Needed one. The taste she'd had last night made her wish for the whole meal.

She tipped her head back into the stream from one shower head. Another one sprayed her front. His cabin was relatively small, but the amenities were first-rate. She squirted shampoo into her palm, closed her eyes, then lathered her hair leisurely, enjoying the steamy spray bathing her everywhere, more aware of her body than she'd ever been. Unhurried, she rinsed the shampoo, feeling it trail her spine. She opened her eyes to look for the soap—and saw Luke.

He stood in the doorway watching her through the crystal-clear glass of the oversize shower stall. She didn't move. They'd made love in the dark last night, exploring without seeing. Nothing was hidden from him now.

She suddenly wished for a more voluptuous body and the ability to look sultry. She didn't care that he didn't want to ruin their relationship with sex. How could anything that felt so good, that seemed so right, ruin what they had?

The soap rested in a recessed holder. She picked it up, stepped out of the spray and soaped herself. He leaned against the doorjamb, his jaw hardening, his gaze heated and direct. Ignoring the facecloth hanging from a hook, she bathed herself using her hands, wishing they were his.

Luke knew he should just leave. He hadn't expected to find her in his shower. Still, he was frozen in place watching her, whether or not he had the right. He'd touched her plenty last night, but seeing her was different. Bubbles clung to her nipples, quivering with each movement, threatening to slip to the ground, but somehow staying there as she circled the bar around her stomach, down her abdomen and into the nest of blond curls that turned white with foam. He hadn't intended to sleep with her again. He didn't think he could avoid it now. He'd stayed too long watching. There wasn't a forgivable excuse in the world if he walked away.

But he couldn't just drag her out of the shower and press her into the bed. He needed more finesse than that, couldn't let himself get too carried away, or else he'd never let her go back home. The plan he'd created was workable. He had to stick to it.

But. She was naked and he was hard with need. Would it really hurt to enjoy each other once more?

"Want company?" he asked.

Trying not to show her relief, Ariel nodded. After a moment's hesitation, he stripped and stood there in all his splendid nakedness, his need unhidden.

Her confidence returned. And something else hovered, as well, something indefinable and meant to stay that way. She was getting in way too deep here. She knew it. She couldn't stop it. Wouldn't stop it.

The shower door clicked opened and the stall got wonderfully crowded.

"That was quite a show, darlin'," he said, pulling her close. He brushed his unshaved cheek against hers, rubbed his bristly jaw in that sensitive spot below her ear, found her mouth and teased her with almost-kisses as his hands curved over her rear and held her against him.

Unable to draw a deep breath, she panted, the lack of oxygen making her light-headed, off-balance. She needed his kiss, a real kiss, a long, dangerous, hot kiss that branded her as his. Still, he teased and tormented with whiskery scrapes and an occasional sweep of his tongue.

She locked her arms behind his neck and hauled herself

up, settling her mouth hard against his, seeking more than just intimacy, but a connection that went beyond that somehow.

"Is this payback?" she breathed between torturous kisses.

He arched her back and trailed his mouth down her throat, between her breasts, then around her nipple, without touching the pebbled crest. "For teasin' me with that soapy hands routine?"

She gasped as he sucked her nipple into his mouth, hard.

"For knowin' no man could've walked away from the temptation?"

"I didn't know. Not for sure," she managed to say before he toyed with the other nipple, his teeth scraping gently. "Lucas. You're driving me wild."

"That's the plan, darlin'. That's definitely the plan."

He slid a hand down low between them, the pad of his thumb swirling, pressing, tormenting, drawing everything from her in a burst of sensation that was almost too strong to enjoy. She didn't have a chance to savor the feeling before he sank to the tiles below and settled his mouth on her. Shocked, she grabbed his hair and held on as he sent pleasure reeling through her again and again. Then while she wasn't able to think one logical thought he pulled her down with him, on him, until they were joined.

The hot water tank drained. Cooling water doused them as she rode him, loving the feel of him filling her, stretching her. Already exhaustingly satisfied herself, she watched him find the pleasure himself, watched the muscles of his face grow taut, watched his jaw clench, watched his eyes close. She felt the warmth of him spill inside her, bringing tears to her eyes with the beauty of the moment, and a little sadness that he couldn't create a new life with that warmth.

"It is damned cold in here," he said suddenly, drawing a laugh from her.

They scrambled up, and she stepped out of the shower and into a huge fluffy towel, leaving him to soap and shampoo in the frigid water. She ran into the living room, stoked the fire and opened her towel in front of it, enjoying the heat against her bare skin. She could stay like this all day, she thought. All week. All month. All year! She'd never felt so alive.

A few minutes later she returned to the bedroom. Luke was already dressed in jeans and boots, and was shaving. He looked at her in the mirror as she leaned against the doorjamb, then he dried his face and reached for the flannel shirt hanging from a nearby hook.

Disappointed at his indifference, Ariel left. She dressed in the guest room, blow dried her hair, then headed for the kitchen. He was already chopping up ham for their omelets.

"Tea'll be done in a couple of minutes," he said. "I poured you a glass of orange juice."

"Thanks." She opened the refrigerator and pulled out the eggs. She didn't know what to say. Thanks for the sex? I needed it. Why don't you ever let me touch you? You're holding back—but why? Are you in that much pain—or are you afraid of hurting me? I'm not so easily broken, you know.

The litany ran through her head without her giving voice to it. Once again her confidence faded. She wasn't used to that. And the unfamiliar always brought confusion.

He touched her arm, bringing her out of her thoughts. "What?" she asked.

"You asked about my fiancées. I'd like to tell you."

Nine

Luke watched her for reaction. He was not comfortable sharing this part of his life. It made him seem like a loser, having been engaged twice without anything coming of it. He steeled himself. *Here goes.*

"You don't have to, Lucas."

He blew out the breath he'd been holding. Huh? What did she mean, he didn't have to? Last night she was dying to know all the details. He watched her beat the eggs, her back to him, then dump the contents in a heated skillet. "I don't?"

"Of course not. It's really none of my business."

Luke frowned. "But I want to tell you."

She looked over her shoulder at him, her eyes sparkling. "Well, if you really want to."

"Are you manipulatin' me, darlin'?"

"Maybe. A little."

"Maybe a lot."

"You just looked so serious. I'm trying to lighten the

mood. We all have pasts, Lucas, good, bad or otherwise. I'm not going to pass judgment on you."

He sat at the kitchen table. "Mary Beth Mabry. She was the first."

"The first fiancée?"

"The first everything."

"What was she like?"

He struggled to recall an image of Mary Beth at eighteen. "A cheerleader."

"I guess that gives me a picture. Bubbly, popular, cute."

"Perky," he said. "Definitely perky. Now, don't you be lookin' at me like that. I was talkin' about her personality."

"Uh-huh. So, what happened?"

"I was raised to respect women, you understand. I wasn't supposed to sleep with one I wasn't gonna make a commitment to. We fooled around a lot, but we didn't do the deed until I couldn't stand it anymore, and I popped the question without even thinkin' about it. She said yes and had her clothes off before I could catch my breath. Helluva night, I can tell you."

Ariel cut the omelet and slid the sections onto plates, then carried them to the table. "In the back of your pickup, I suppose?"

"Nope. Outdoors, though. Got a bunch of mosquito bites, as I recall." He took a bite of egg and chewed. "I was home from college for the summer, although I had to go back early because of bein' a football player. By the time I left, we'd called it quits. The sex was great, but otherwise we didn't have anything to talk about. Her second child is my godson."

"Is she still perky?"

"She's a real nice lady, Ariel. We just weren't suited. The man she married gave her a nice home and four kids, just like she wanted."

He looked away when he mentioned the children. He couldn't give Mary Beth what she'd wanted, his words implied. Worked out all around. "And fiancée number two?" she asked.

"Now, this is a mite darker tale of love gone wrong. Olivia Adams. We went together my last two years of college, got engaged when I was drafted to the Dusters. She kept movin' the wedding date, though, puttin' it back again and again until finally she gave me back the ring."

"Why?"

"Olivia had grown up poor and had expensive tastes. I found out eventually that she was lookin' for financial security. Figured if she had a couple of kids with me, given my potential as a pro, she could be set for life. Marry me, then divorce me down the road, live on child support."

Ariel set down her fork. "That's terrible."

"Could've been worse. Could've married her, after all. She was only the second woman I'd slept with—I'm a real monogamous man, in case you're wonderin'. I confused lust with love. I didn't see what she was up to. A few of my friends tried to tell me. A couple even said they'd seen her out with other guys in a neighboring town. I didn't want to believe it. To me, when you're committed, you're true. Period."

"You haven't changed your mind about that, I hope."

"It jaded me for a while after, I admit. I'm not proud of it. But I settled down soon enough. She'd played me for a fool, though. I almost had the last laugh when we found out I was sterile."

If it hadn't hurt so much, that is. Ariel completed the sentence. And it had hurt him. Still hurt him. "How did you? Why did you even check?"

"She'd been tryin' for over two years to trap me. She never got pregnant."

"Were you tested? Maybe the problem was with her."

"I got tested because she asked me to. I figured, why not? I didn't know her plans, of course. Didn't know why she wanted me to get myself checked. She worked at a doctor's office, and she showed me the results. Hell, she got herself pregnant by another of my teammates shortly thereafter, had herself two kids and lives on child support now, just like she planned. Not a pretty story, is it?''

Ariel reached across the table to touch the back of his hand.

''Anyway,'' he said, cutting into his omelet again, ''the point is, I've dated a lot, but I haven't slept around a lot. I wanted you to know.''

''Why?''

''Well, you trusted me with what eats at you the most, right?''

Ariel stuffed food in her mouth. Guilt swamped her. She hadn't told him everything. She wouldn't—couldn't—tell him everything. He didn't have a need to know. No one ever would.

''So, darlin', are you gonna tell me about your first time?''

''A lady never kisses and tells.''

He grinned. ''That bad, huh?''

''Actually, it was...pleasant.''

''Pleasant? Pleasant is for tea parties. You can do better than that.''

''What can I say?'' She sipped her tea, fondly remembering a night almost ten years ago—and Jean-Claude. ''He was gentle. It was nice.''

''Nice. Shoot, Ariel. Nice?''

'''Nice' is good for a first time.'' She carried her plate to the sink, then walked back to him. He'd pushed his chair back to clear his own dishes. She straddled his lap, looped her arms around his neck and kissed him. ''You didn't make me feel nice, Lucas.''

He frowned.

She loosened his shirt buttons as she kissed him again, slid her hands under the fabric and into the soft hair covering his chest. She didn't know why hairy chests had always been such a turn-off to her before. She loved his.

''You just made me *feel*,'' she said.

I'm weak, Luke thought, as he slipped his hands under the back of her sweater, finding her naked underneath. All this talk about sex had him more excited than a kid seein' his first girlie magazine. Couldn't have anything at all to do with the woman sucking his ear lobe into her mouth and—

Growling? Ariel? His Miz Wholesome?

He chuckled. He couldn't help it. She was just so different from how he had her figured.

"What are you laughing about?" she asked, angling back.

"I don't know if I'm laughin' so much as I'm more kinda enjoyin' you. You aren't what I expected."

"Exactly what did you expect?"

"Now, don't get all huffy on me." He shifted his legs a little as they started to go numb. "I'm not tryin' to get you to move, either. Just settlin' you more comfortably. Frankly, darlin', I knew you were a friendly person and that you're always workin' for the social good. But I didn't expect you to be the sexually demandin' type."

"You expected some kind of untouchable princess?"

"I s'pose. Kind of."

"Well, I'm so sorry to disappoint you."

"Didn't say I was disappointed. Said I was surprised."

"Well then, let me clarify everything for you." She framed his face with her hands and kissed him. "I'm going to be very demanding of you."

"I'm quiverin' with fear at the thought."

She laughed, soft and low. "As well you should be." She swept his lower lip with her tongue. Their breaths mingled, caressing hotly. Teasing. Promising.

The phone rang, an obscenity of sound in the quietness of their hideaway and the electrically charged moment of anticipation.

"I have to get that," he said. "It can only be an emergency."

Luke helped her move off his lap, then made his way to the telephone and said hello.

"Mr. Walker, this is Dr. Morningstar."

Uh-oh. "Shannon, how are you?"

"Don't you 'Shannon' me, pal. You didn't show up for surgery."

"I left you a message Sunday night."

"You were supposed to be in surgery Monday morning, Luke. You can't just cancel the night before."

"I had to." He watched Ariel keep busy by washing the dishes. "I was wiped out. Needed to get away."

"You were wiped out? That warrants canceling surgery—again?"

He held the phone away as she screeched the last word.

"Mr. Walker, I've been very patient with you. You haven't followed my instructions well. I'll bet you've left your crutches at home yet again and have totally ruined what was your better knee. Am I right?"

"Not totally. I don't think."

She muttered a string of curses that made him nostalgic for the team locker room. He could hear her grit her teeth as she got the next sentence out.

"Since I can't trust you to show up in the morning, I expect you to check yourself into the hospital by ten o'clock tonight so that you can go under the knife—"

Luke winced. She'd used the phrase intentionally.

"Or else I'm resigning as your doctor. See how long it'll take you to have that knee fixed then."

He could've gotten another surgeon easily, Luke figured. Celebrity had its rewards. But the point was, he had confidence in Shannon. Liked her, too. Hell, she'd been on his wife list, he recalled. At the moment he wondered why, though. She was really too bossy. Strident. Grating, even.

"Do you hear me, Luke?"

"I do, Shannon. I'll be there."

"No excuses?"

"I'll be there," he repeated impatiently. He was only trying to get his entire future settled, for God's sake. He needed to be left alone to do that.

"Problem?" Ariel asked when he hung up.

"Yeah. I'm sorry to tell you this, but we're gonna have

to pack up and go now. I've got to be back home by ten o'clock tonight."

"Trouble at work?"

He hesitated. "Yeah. Can't wait until tomorrow."

She folded the dish towel over a rack. "Who's Shannon?"

"An associate. How fast can you be ready?"

"Depends on how much cleanup we have to do. The beds aren't made, even."

"Leave 'em. My caretaker will clean." He walked to where she stood leaning against the counter, her arms folded. "I'm sorry."

"Me, too. It was nice while it lasted."

She looked so dejected, he took her in his arms and held her. "Nice, huh? There's that word again."

"I'm not sure how much rest we got, for all that it was our intention in coming here."

"We would've had to leave in five or six hours, anyway, so we could both be back at work tomorrow morning."

"I know. It's just that I had plans for those five or six hours."

"Sleepin', I s'pose."

"A nap would've been part of my plans. After."

"You wear me out, just thinkin' about it."

"There's another solution, Lucas."

"What's that?"

"We could stay here another few hours, then I could just drop you off where you live and drive myself back to San Francisco."

He loosened his hold and moved back a little. "I have to get my jet home."

"I know. Couldn't you just hire someone to bring it back?"

"You can't start worryin' about me flyin'. The plane's manufacturer has an excellent safety record. I have a top-notch mechanic. And I'm a good pilot."

"I was just trying to figure out a way to stay here longer."

He lifted her chin, making her look him in the eye. "I'll

be all right, Ariel. I don't want you gettin' all worked up about it."

"Fine." She walked away and headed for the bedroom. "I guess we'd better get on the road, then."

Luke sighed. *Looks like the trip back is gonna be as much fun as the trip up.* Lord but that woman knew how to keep a man on his toes.

"You're so serious," Ariel said to Luke. They'd just finished eating dinner, having picked up Chinese takeout at a restaurant near her apartment when they got back into the city. Actually, he seemed more nervous than serious, Ariel decided. He hadn't eaten much. He hadn't been able to sit still, having gotten up from the sofa several times in the past twenty minutes to get something from the kitchen or, once, from his jacket pocket.

"I have a question to ask you," he replied, rubbing his hands along his thighs. He stuck a hand in his pants' pocket and brought out a small dark blue velvet box. He stared at it a minute, then pushed up the lid and turned it so that she could see the contents.

A very large diamond ring winked at her as if saying, "Ha! I knew his secret before you."

She swallowed and looked up at him.

"I'm asking you to marry me, Ariel."

"You're not serious."

"On the contrary, I couldn't be more serious."

"Why?"

"What do you mean *why?* Why does any man ask a woman to marry him?"

"It's a perfectly logical question. We hardly know each other. And I've already told you that marriage isn't in my plans. Why are you putting me on the spot like this?" She stood abruptly, needing to get away from the ring he'd taken out of the case and held now between his thumb and forefinger, as if he could just slide it right on her hand, branding her as his. "Tell me why you're asking."

"Because I want you to be my wife, of course. I think we suit very well."

"After six days, you've come to the decision that we could spend the rest of our lives together?"

"We're sexually compatible, we like each other, and I don't think you'd object to adopting kids. I know all I need to know."

It was easier to argue with him than to dissect her feelings right then—and the fact he wasn't mentioning love…

"I don't have time for a family, Lucas. I have too much to do, too many others in need. I can't spread myself that thin or everything would suffer. I've found my place in life. A place where I can help hundreds of people have better lives."

"Does that keep you warm at night? Does that provide you with children to care for you in your old age? Grandchildren to love?"

"I don't need a family to be fulfilled." She crossed her arms as he came up to her.

"Don't need a family? Hell, darlin', you gather little families everywhere you go. What do you call the people at the senior citizens center, or the kids at the youth center, or the symphony you saved from bankruptcy with that charity cruise where we met? And those are just the ones I'm aware of. You're lookin' for home. Home and family and continuity. Just like me."

She shook her head. He'd come too close to the truth for her to say otherwise.

"Don't lie to yourself, Ariel. There isn't any continuity in your life except for what you create—and that can change at any time, because the bonds are superficial. For all the people in your life, you're lonely. Admit it."

"I'm not in the least lonely. A lot of people depend on me. I'm busy from morning to night. I don't have time to be lonely."

"There's no denyin' that what you give people is important. But isn't it only the outcome that matters, not who does the job? You bring something special to it all, I'll grant you that. But what do you get? There isn't the real bond of family, of permanence.''

''Permanence is a myth,'' she countered, walking away. She regretted having told him about losing her family. He was using it to make a point she couldn't ever agree with. ''Death comes without warning. Couples split up. Nothing's permanent. I've found what I need, what never disappoints me.''

''What won't leave you.''

The truth hurt. She didn't want him to see how much. ''I have a purpose in life. I warned you about that.''

Luke forced himself to remain calm. In actuality, he wasn't surprised by her refusal. But he'd planted the seed in her mind now. He could let it take root awhile, then nurture it along. Given a little time and tenderness, it'd grow and blossom. A *little* time, mind you. He had to get his new life started.

''You can continue your charity work, Ariel. In fact, I'll put you in charge of Titan's philanthropic funds. You could probably help a lot more people than you do now.''

''Don't dangle that carrot at me. I've got the means to help as many people as I want. I just happen to prefer personal contact, not some corporate decision culminating in a check.''

''It'd be your choice completely. You can scout out each project yourself.''

''Oh, I see now. You're determined to make me get on an airplane, because there's no way I could drive myself far enough to investigate, otherwise.''

''Fears should be challenged. Conquered. But that has nothing to do with my proposin' marriage to you. I'm ready for a family. I think you are, too.''

''Third fiancée's not the charm, Lucas,'' she announced. ''And if you think that—that *ring* you're holding is right for me, then you don't know me at all. It's just proof of how right I am.''

"What's wrong with this ring? The jeweler said it's a flawless diamond. Three carats. Perfect."

"A perfect ring should only go to a perfect woman. I'm not it." She frowned. "Where'd you come up with that, anyway? And when?"

"Ariel." He set his hands on her shoulders.

She pulled away. "Damn you, Lucas. You ruined everything! I can't even sleep with you again, knowing you want to marry me. How could you do that?"

"Only you would consider it a crime to make an honest woman of you." He shook his head. "What had you expected of this relationship?"

"That we'd get together every so often for a weekend or something. Talk on the phone during the week, maybe. You know."

"You mean, you'd be happy just havin' sex with me and nothin' else?"

She shrugged uncomfortably.

He pushed a little harder. "You just wanted to use me as your boy toy or something? Ariel Minx, you are one cruel lady."

"Stop making fun of me."

"Darlin', if I was only guessin' before that you were the right woman for me, I know for sure now." He laughed, then he swept her into his arms and kissed her, intending to leave her breathless and speechless. Then he said goodbye.

"You're not getting the last word," she called out the door as he walked to the rental car that Sam and Marguerite had left for him.

He turned around and walked backward. It killed his knee. "Go ahead."

"I despise you."

"No, you don't."

He could almost see steam coming out her ears.

"Don't call me, because I won't talk to you."

"Yes, you will."

"You are completely resistible."

"To most women, maybe." He grinned. "But not to you."

"Someone has to say no to you."

"Won't be you," he said, reaching the car.

"I already have!"

He unlocked the door, then just before he slid into the car, he said, "I wonder how many times you said yes last night and this morning, darlin'. I didn't count, but—"

"Go away." Ariel looked around to see if any of her neighbors were around. She was either going to laugh or cry within the next ten seconds. She didn't want him to see it. "And don't come back."

She shut the door. She thought she heard him say something, but since she hadn't heard for sure, she decided he hadn't gotten the last word in. So she won—a very small battle. Ha!

Then she sat on her sofa and burst into tears.

He didn't know what he'd done. She buried her face in a pillow and screamed. She'd blocked the idea of having a normal life, a family, since she was a child. Her role was predetermined, her path set.

Now he'd dropped a little glimmer of something else into it, created a fork in the road with a rainbow leading to some kind of pot of gold he'd manufactured—a family.

How could she take the new path and still fulfill her destiny?

Maybe. If he loved her…

Wouldn't he have said so, though? He seemed to be offering her some kind of business deal. He knew she'd be willing to adopt children. He knew she wanted an intimate—a sexual—relationship. He knew she'd love to get her hands on Titan's money to help people in need. Oh, he knew all the right buttons to push.

She was just push-button resistant.

Ten

"All I want to know is if you can put a fake name on the lab test, Shannon," Luke said. He stood staring out the hospital window, unable to see the mountains in the night sky. "I'd like to have it done before the surgery tomorrow."

"I'm an orthopedic surgeon," Shannon replied. "You don't think someone will figure out if I order a sperm count, that it's yours, no matter whose name is on the label?"

He turned around. "I hadn't thought of that."

"It's a small community, Luke. I wouldn't count on confidentiality. You're big news around here. Your best bet is to have your GP order one for you after you get home. He can assign it a number."

"Okay. Thanks."

She sat on the edge of his bed, his chart tucked under her arm. "Are you checking DNA? Has someone filed a paternity suit against you?"

"Nope. In fact, I'm pretty sure I'm sterile. But I realized I never had it confirmed myself and I should, I suppose. I mean, someone told me, but she lied about a lot of things. I should verify it, right?"

"You've just guessed you're sterile? Yeah, I'd say you should check it out." She cocked her head. "You're certainly subdued tonight."

Luke took a seat in the only chair in the room. He hated hospitals. Had spent too much time in them, not just for his own injuries but with friends and teammates through the years. Football was brutal on a body.

"I've been through a lot lately," he said. "If I can't unwind with a friend, what good is having one?"

"Am I your friend?" she asked.

"I thought you were." *Hell, you were on my wife list. I had to have felt something for you,* he thought. But he couldn't picture anyone in that role now except Ariel.

"If we're friends, Luke, you have a strange way of showing it."

"Meanin' what, exactly?"

"I mean, if you wanted to know details about me, you could've just asked. Hiring a private investigator was completely unnecessary. My life's an open book."

Damn. He'd forgotten to cancel the background check on the wife candidates.

"I'm sorry. It was a mistake, Shannon. I hope he didn't disturb you."

"I wasn't bothered too much, but Victoria went ballistic. I expect you'll be hearing from her."

"Victoria?"

"Your lawyer?" she prompted. "Also, my significant other."

He blinked, surprised. "Oh. I didn't know." Scratch two more off the list. The thought made him laugh. He'd screwed up this project from the beginning. It wasn't over yet, though. Ariel was bein' balky, but nothing he couldn't handle.

"You want to tell me why we were subjected to a background check?"

"Not really, Doc. I'd sound stupider than ever. I promise

I'll tell you why later, but someone else needs to hear it first. Just so you know, though, I wasn't lookin' for a lot of details, only some real basic information."

"I'll accept that."

He laughed again. "Thanks. You're a helluva woman."

"So I've been told. Victoria's a different matter altogether, though, Luke." She stood. She laid a hand on his shoulder when she reached his chair. "We'll get you fixed up tomorrow, then you can get back to an active life again."

He nodded.

When she left, he dialed Ariel's house.

"Just wanted to let you know I'm home, safe and sound."

Silence greeted him, then an abrupt and snippy, "Thanks."

He wished she was there. He wished someone was there to keep him distracted and make him laugh. He could call his cousin, but Sam was undoubtedly with Marguerite. "Ariel?"

"What?"

"I had a great time this week."

She answered with a put-upon sigh. "Me, too. Until the last few minutes."

"If I don't mention marriage again for a while, can I call you?"

"Lucas—"

"Pretty please."

He could tell she was trying not to laugh.

"Okay, okay. But the *M* word is off limits—and not just for a while. For*ever*."

He relaxed against the pillows and stretched out his legs. "You would be willin' to adopt kids, though, right?"

"Lucas!"

He held the phone away from his ear for a second. "What? It's not the *M* word."

"Good night, Mr. Walker."

The phone went dead. He cradled the receiver and smiled. Kids. She loved kids. He could get to her that way. He never even had to bring up marriage again. At some point, she'd be askin' *him.*

He punched Marguerite's phone number.

"I thought I'd let you know that I'm at the hospital," he said when she answered. "I'll be in surgery first thing in the morning. If it goes like last time, I'll be home tomorrow afternoon and back in the office on Thursday. How's my schedule?"

"It's clear. How come you're not yelling at me for giving your cabin number to Dr. Morningstar?"

"I'm feelin' way too mellow to yell at anybody. I want a dozen red roses delivered to Ariel tomorrow, and—"

"No."

Luke paused. "No?"

"Ariel Minx is not a red roses kind of woman, Luke. Try again."

"I thought all women liked—"

"I'm putting you on the speaker. Sam, talk to your cousin. Explain the facts of life to him."

"Hey, Luke," Sam said, his voice tinny over the speaker.

Luke could hear the grin. "My dad gave me The Birds and Bees lecture a long time ago."

"Then consider this The Care and Handling of Women lecture. This goes beyond sex, cousin."

"I have a feelin' this is gonna sound a lot like Marguerite."

Sam chuckled. "Women are not interchangeable. Having met the lady in question, I have to admit I agree with Marguerite. Ariel isn't red roses."

Luke rubbed at the ache settling in his forehead. "I knew that. I just didn't think about it." He had to do something about being so goal oriented. He wasn't seeing the forest for the trees.

He closed his eyes and thought about Ariel. "Daisies, maybe. Or orchids," he said with more enthusiasm. "You know, those little bitty orchids they have in the hotel rooms in Hawaii. The ones that look fragile but they're not. Yeah.

That's Ariel. Marguerite, have some shipped in, please. A lot of them."

"A tasteful few dozen," Marguerite said, brooking no argument. "There's hope for you, after all, Luke. What do you want written on the card?"

"Hell. I have to put something besides my name?" He could hear Sam laughing. "Shut up. You were a sap, too, when you were courtin' Marguerite. Just put, 'These remind me of you.'"

When he hung up, he put the phone aside, turned out the lights and stared out the window for a long time. He still had a lot to learn. Roses were wrong. Diamonds were wrong. What else was he wrong about? He'd never treated any woman differently from another before. None of them had complained.

He winced. How chauvinistic did *that* sound?

He dragged the telephone into his lap again and dialed.

"H'lo?"

She sounded sleepy and sexy all at the same time. No wonder he had so much trouble figurin' her out. She never was just one thing or another that he could label, but a combination of lots of things.

"Ariel."

"Lucas?" He could hear the bed coverings rustle and a lamp click on. "What's wrong?"

He shut his eyes. He wanted her beside him so much it hurt, like a vise grip squeezing him everywhere. "I wasn't honest with you today."

"About what?"

"That call I got at the cabin today was my doctor. My surgeon, that is. I'm calling you from the hospital. I'm going to have surgery on my knee tomorrow. It's no big deal. I don't know why I just didn't tell you."

"Because you're such a tough guy."

Luke smiled at the gently teasing tone. "Yeah."

"Do you want me to be there? Is that why you're calling?"

"No. Your schedule's full. I know it's hard to rearrange things. I just..."

"What?"

"I just missed you."

She said his name. Just his name. But the way she said it...

"Don't be mad at me, Ariel."

"I'm not mad." She sighed. "I'm just ticked off."

"Oh. Well, thanks for clarifyin' that. I was worried."

She laughed. "You're a charming bulldozer, Lucas Walker."

"You think I'm charmin'?"

"Don't forget the bulldozer part. That's important, too."

Relaxed finally, he couldn't keep his eyes open. "The sleepin' pill they gave me is knockin' me out, darlin', so I'd better hang up. I'll call you tomorrow."

"Call my cellular phone. I'll have it turned on all day. Good luck tomorrow, Lucas."

"Thanks. I'll be seein' you."

He hung up, wishing he'd told her yes, that he wanted her to be with him. It had nothing to do with the surgery, however.

Pulling up the covers, he yawned. He had a lot to think about now.

A lot...

Ariel perused the report Chase Ryan handed her. She was sitting in his office at the youth center, having stopped there before picking up the meals to deliver.

"How will you earmark the funds?" she asked Chase, who sat across from her, behind his desk.

"I never expected to have so much to work with. Maybe we should make a wish list, then take a vote."

"You wanted to get some computers," Ariel said, eyeing her watch. Why hadn't he called? He should have called by now.

"Your friend Luke donated a whole bunch of computers

that his company just replaced. With a little cash investment, we can upgrade them well enough to be up-to-date for now.''

''You're kidding.''

''They should be arriving by the middle of next week.''

''Why'd he do that? How did he know?''

''He talked to the kids, asked them what kinds of equipment they'd like to have. He probably meant sports equipment. I think they surprised him. Am I keeping you from something, Ariel?''

''What?'' He'd caught her checking her watch again. ''No. I'm just waiting for a phone call. Lucas had knee surgery this morning. He was supposed to call.''

On cue, her phone chirped. She said hello before the second ring.

''Hi.''

''Did everything go okay?'' she asked, aware of Chase leaving the room, giving her privacy.

''There was a little more damage than they'd anticipated, but, yeah, it's okay. Had to scrape some old scar tissue away as well as repair the injury. Surgery took longer than I expected.''

''So what happens now?''

''Sam's here. He's takin' me home.''

''I suppose you'll be back at work tomorrow.''

''It hasn't affected my mind, darlin',' he said, a smile in his voice. ''I'll just prop up my leg.''

''Call me later?''

''Sure thing.''

''Mind the doctor's orders, Lucas.''

''I promise.''

Ariel flipped the phone shut and held it with both hands, as if it connected her with him somehow. She should be there taking care of him, making sure he took his medicine and rested and ate well.

She sighed. This was worse than she thought.

''Did the surgery go okay?'' Chase asked when he returned.

"So he says."

He contemplated her for a few seconds, then opened a desk drawer and pulled out a newspaper. "I know you were out of town for a couple of days. Did you see this?"

"More publicity for the Center?" Ariel reached for it, focusing on the photograph front and center of her and Luke at the Super Bowl. The picture had been taken at the moment when they'd had their arms around each other after he'd waved to the crowd. Someone using a telephoto lens from across the stadium had captured the embrace. The caption identified the city's most eligible bachelor with his mystery lady, naming her.

"Well. At least they spelled my name right," she said to Chase. Her voice sounded an octave higher and a few decibels softer than usual, even to her.

"Is this going to cause you problems?" he asked.

"I don't know." She folded the paper carefully and tucked it into her purse. "I really don't know."

"What can I do, Ariel?"

She shook her head. "Nothing. I just have to wait and see."

"If you need a place to go, all you have to do is ask. My apartment upstairs is very secure."

She smiled a little. "I'm not a criminal or anything, Chase. The reason I stay out of the spotlight is personal. Extremely personal. I knew I was taking a big risk by going out with someone who's such a public figure. My hormones staged an all-out mutiny against my common sense."

"It had to be more than just your hormones involved for you to take that kind of a chance. You chose to be in public with him."

"Who understands a woman's mind?" she asked wryly.

"Certainly not me." He leaned toward her. "My offer holds. If you need me for anything, I'll be here."

She stood. She had to think about the consequences of the publicity. How long would she have to wait before she could relax? "I've got to go. Thanks, Chase. You're a good friend."

When she arrived home that evening, she locked the door behind her and walked into the bedroom to check her answering machine, although she didn't know what she was expecting. Her number was unlisted. Any messages would be from friends.

The light wasn't flashing. Relieved, she sank to the edge of the bed, not realizing how tense she was until she relaxed. A hot bath would do the rest, she decided.

The phone rang.

Her heart started pounding. "Hello?"

"Hi."

She closed her eyes and clutched the receiver. "How's the patient?"

"Crabby, in pain, and not a lot of fun to be around. Did I catch you at a bad time?"

"I just got home. Um, do you get the San Francisco newspaper?"

"Just on Sunday. Why?"

"There's a picture of us in Monday's paper." She described it to him. "How do you suppose they got my name?"

"From someone in the owner's box, I expect."

He didn't say I told you so, but his inflection implied it. "You warned me, I guess. And the media are determined and single-minded. I know that from ex—" She caught herself. "Examples I see every day."

"Are you upset about it?"

She had to think about it. *Upset* wasn't the right word, but she wasn't sure what was. "I guess not."

"We're probably old news by now," he said.

"You're probably right. So, are you really going to work tomorrow? Shouldn't you be resting at least one full day?"

"I can rest in the office just as well as I can at home. I've got a lot of work piled up, waiting. Maybe I'll go in for only a few hours. Ariel?"

"Hmm?"

"I'm tryin' to change."

"What do you mean?"

"I mean, I realized I don't know the first thing about bein' a husband. I'm not surprised you turned me down, 'cause it's obvious, now that I've looked closer."

"Oh, Lucas. There's nothing wrong with you. Nothing."

"Then why did you turn me down?"

"Not because of you. It's me. I tried to explain."

"Could you ever get past my bein' a pilot? Is that a deal breaker?"

"It's not that simple. Why can't we just have a relationship? Why does it have to get so complicated? I can make room in my life for you. I just can't make room for a full-time life with you, because that includes too much else with it."

"You're not capable of havin' only a relationship, and you know it. It's all or nothing with you. I'm just figurin' that out. Good night, Ariel."

He didn't even wait for her to say anything, but just hung up. Ariel tried to decide if she was angry or amused. So, he'd been giving her a lot of thought, had he? If that meant he was going to treat her differently, she didn't want it. She liked who he was. She liked that he struggled to be sensitive and understanding when his nature was to shrug things off and go on. Not that he hadn't been sensitive and understanding when she'd told him about the plane crash, but that was different. That was a momentous event, not daily life.

The phone rang. Expecting Luke, she said, "Good night to you, too."

A pause, then, "Ariel?"

"Chase?"

"Yeah. Sorry. You were expecting someone else. Should I call back?"

"Um, no." She felt her cheeks heat. "What's up?"

"A private investigator was here today asking questions about you."

As fast as she'd turned hot, she turned cold now. "What kinds of questions?"

"He started off asking about the Center in general, then about me, then about how we're funded, which led to the Angel Foundation. Which led to you."

"Who was the investigator? Luke ordered a background check before he let Titan come aboard," Ariel said hopefully. "Maybe because the company is getting even more involved, he wants more information."

"His name is Douglas Jett. He had the newspaper articles mentioning you as the mystery lady, and the photograph with Luke. What bothered me was how much more intense he was when he questioned me about you. I told him nothing, of course, but I made sure I didn't get defensive with him, otherwise he might think I knew a secret he should uncover."

"I'll ask Luke about it. Thanks for letting me know."

She depressed the receiver and dialed Luke. She could tell when he answered that he'd been asleep.

"I'm sorry to wake you."

"'S'all right, darlin'. What can I do for you?"

"Remember the P.I. you hired to check out the Center? Was his name Douglas Jett?"

"Nope. Jerry Meyer. Why?"

"Is he independent or with a firm?"

"Independent. I used to play ball with him. What's goin' on?"

She closed her eyes. Now what? "Um, someone needed a recommendation. So, you think he's good?"

"He's thorough. Loves a puzzle better than anything. He always had his nose stuck in a mystery when we were on the road."

"Okay, thanks. Go back to sleep."

He chuckled. "Yes, ma'am."

Ariel cradled the phone. She looked around her bedroom, seeing the world she'd created for herself. Secure, isolated, comfortable. How long did she have before all that was shattered?

Eleven

Luke shut the car door and looked up at Ariel's apartment. The place was lit up. Good. They hadn't seen each other for two weeks, although they talked on the phone at least once a day. Something was going on with her, though. She had become less communicative, less lively, less…Ariel. He'd been immersed in the most important project of his career and hadn't been able to get away the past two weekends to see her, so he'd decided to fly down on a weeknight and surprise her. Ariel, of all people, would love surprises.

Like James Bond approaching a nunnery, he padded up the stairs, pulling out his cell phone at the same time and punching in her number.

"Hello?"

"If you've got company, darlin', you'd best kick 'em out right now."

"Hi, to you, too. And I'm alone. Why? Got a little phone sex planned, Lucas?"

"Now, there's a thought. What are you wearin'?"

"Nothing."

"Seriously?" He rang her doorbell.

"My birthday suit and a smile," she said, then, "You're on my porch!"

"I am?"

"I can see you through the peephole. What are you—"

The door opened with a whoosh.

"Liar." He leaned against the doorjamb.

She stood there, a smile lighting up her face.

"You're not wearin' your birthday suit." He snapped his phone closed and dropped it into his suit pocket. "I like what you've got on almost as much, though."

"What are you doing here?"

"Takin' you out to dinner, if you're willin' to get out of that slinky little thing you call a robe and into something fancy." She was dewy and pink-cheeked, as if she'd just emerged from a long, hot bubble bath. Her hair, piled mostly on top of her head, was damp along her hairline. He plucked her cordless phone from her, pressed the Power switch off and tossed it onto the sofa, then hauled her into his arms.

"Lord, I missed you," he said just before he settled his mouth on hers.

He didn't meet resistance. Her arms twined his neck instantly and locked behind his head. Her mouth tasted like heaven, the little moans floating up from her throat tickled his tongue. He'd forgotten how good she felt, how perfectly she fit with him.

Feeling a change in her, a withdrawal, he lifted his head. She burrowed against his chest, stifling a sound he suspected was a sob. "Here, now. What's this? Tears?"

"I'm sorry. They caught me off guard, too. I don't think I knew how much I missed you until I saw you," she said against his chest, her arms tight around him. "I've been kind of emotional lately."

So, in the end it had worked out well, his leaving her alone. She'd come to appreciate him. He pulled the band from her hair, then combed the tangles from it with his fingers. "What's goin' on with you?"

"It's just been stressful lately."

"You do too much."

"There's so much to do." She pushed away from him and turned around, pulling some tissues out of her pocket. "Why didn't you let me know you were coming? What if I hadn't been home?"

"Then it wouldn't have been a surprise, now, would it? And you've been home every night, so I figured the odds were good. This is the first free night I've had, and the last I will have for another week. As soon as I've made my presentation to the board, I'll have time again." He looked around, pleased to see orchids in bowls and vases. "Why don't you slip into a nice dress and I'll take you out on the town."

"I don't know if I'm up to a public date, Lucas."

He stared at the back of her head, noted the tension in her posture. "I've reserved a room at a private club. No one will see us but our waiter, and his job hinges on discretion. I haven't been there before, but I know a few people who have, people who wanted total privacy and got it."

"I could just fix us something here."

"Then I wouldn't get to take you out." He came up behind her, set his hands on her shoulders and turned her around. He didn't like what he saw. "Are you having nightmares again?"

"I've never been a pretty crier, that's all. I just need to splash some cold water on my face. Do you want to help me choose a dress or shall I surprise you?"

"You'd let me pick?"

"There's nothing in my closet I wouldn't feel comfortable wearing."

Ariel sat on her bed and tugged a floppy stuffed basset hound into her lap, one of several gifts Luke had sent. She watched him sort through her clothes, taking dresses out one at a time and inspecting them as if his life depended on choosing the right one. "Too summery, right?" he asked once. "Too pink," he said about another. He finally settled on a short, snug, off-the-shoulder, long-sleeve dress that she could shimmy up her body. It would cling everywhere.

She would have picked it herself, but she was glad he'd made the choice and couldn't accuse her of teasing him by wearing it.

He carried it to her. "This one. It matches your eyes."

"The dress is black, Lucas. My eyes are brown."

"Most times when you look at me, they're black as sin." He laid the dress across the bottom of the bed and sat beside her. "Did you name the dog?"

"I did. I named him after you."

"I'm afraid to ask."

"Posse."

"How's that like me?"

"It's short for Impossible."

"Why, I'm brimmin' with possibilities, darlin', don't you know?" He lifted the gold lid of a box on her nightstand and swiped a chocolate. "I almost sent you salt-water taffy. Then I thought, nope. I'll bet Ariel likes chocolate. It's a sensual kinda candy, isn't it?"

"Orgasmic," she confirmed, enjoying the way his brows raised. "You shouldn't buy me so much, though. You've spent a fortune."

He smiled leisurely. "For every cent I've spent on presents, I've sent the same amount in a check to one of your favorite charities."

"You have?" She laughed, pleased. "When did you get to know me so well?"

"I've been workin' on it awhile."

"I don't know you nearly as much."

"I'm pretty much a what-you-see-is-what-you-get kinda guy. Not very complicated."

"That's not true. I think you're very complex. And fascinating."

"Then I guess my strategy's workin'."

They stared at each other a minute. "I suppose I should change," she said at last. "Are you planning on watching me dress? I have no objection, mind you. I'm just curious."

He traced the vee of her robe with his fingertips, felt the smooth, sloping contour of her breasts, resisted the temptation to push the garment off her shoulders. He met her gaze as he let his hand slip under the silk long enough to remind himself how perfectly her breast fit his palm. "It's probably safer if I mosey on out to the living room."

"Probably."

Her skin was warm and soft and smooth. The womanly shape of her conformed to his hand, and he could no more resist teasing the hard nipple pressing his palm than he could resist kissing her soft, sweet lips. There was nothing to compare to the feel of her—all enticing woman.

He was quiet a long time. She waited.

He finally stood, grasped her hand and pulled her up. "I think I'd like to spend the evening imaginin' what you're wearin' underneath rather than knowin'. I'll wait in the other room."

"Coward."

"And not ashamed to admit it, darlin'."

Luke found himself using a gentler voice as the evening wore on, a softer touch, a quieter kind of humor. Ariel seemed fragile, all of a sudden. Stretched thin. Ready to break. It wasn't just the crying that had made her face seem haggard, but a deep-down tiredness, worse than before, even. Tiredness mixed with...what? He didn't know, and she sure wasn't saying.

When he took his first bite of chocolate mousse something else struck him. In all the madness of the past couple of weeks, he'd forgotten to follow through on his fertility test. Hell. What if he wasn't sterile?

What if she was pregnant?

He put his spoon down deliberately and wiped his mouth with his napkin. She was moaning and sighing over the rich chocolate and not paying attention to the terror striking him. What if, what if, what if? And how could he ask her?

If she was, she'd only be two weeks along. Could she tell that soon? Could *he?* If he'd stayed in the bedroom and seen her naked, maybe he would have seen something— Nah. Impossible.

She was tired, just like she said. That's all. He was sterile. The test would be a formality.

Still. What if?

She'd think he lied to her, to trap her. Aw, hell.

"Are you okay?" she asked, laying her hand on his.

"What? Oh, yeah. I'm fine. Why?"

"You're not eating. And if you don't want your chocolate decadence, I do."

Startled, he just stared at her. Didn't women's appetites increase during pregnancy? No. They got sick. But not all of them. Damn. What was he doing to himself?

"If you want my dessert, you're welcome to it," he said, sliding it her way, then watching her dig into his and start the moaning and sighing routine all over again. He wondered if the waiter would hesitate outside the door, thinking they were making love.

They could, if they wanted to. The door had a lock. The sofa looked big enough. It'd probably seen plenty of action. He was more than a little curious about what she was wearing underneath, because it sure as hell couldn't be much.

Halfway through the first course, he'd given up sneaking peeks at her nipples, which seemed to stay hard all evening. Her shape was revealed perfectly by the smooth, fitted fabric of her dress. Either she'd been cold all night or aroused. The room was well heated, however.

Luke eyed the sofa again, speculating, then discarded the idea. It seemed tawdry, somehow. And he hadn't made the trip to the city with the intention of making love with her.

"So, finish telling me about the project you're working on," she said between bites.

He decided he could use the distraction. "These are all

the ideas I've been putting together for years, includin' the newest one we talked about, shoes targeted for the seniors market. It's my blueprint for the future of Titan. I'm presentin' it to the board of directors next week." He smiled. "Wait'll you see the video we shot with Emma and a few of the other seniors as a promo for the idea. She's a natural."

"I was there when the film crew came in," Ariel said. "She was trying to be so cool, but I could tell how excited she was. Are you worried about how the board will receive your ideas?"

He thought about the image problem he had with the board, thanks to the efficient work of his publicist throughout his football career. He thought about the year-to-year contract he had, and how he had more to prove than another man might because he wasn't being taken seriously, given his background, as well as being the grandson of the CEO, a fact which only complicated matters. "I just want to do well."

"I wouldn't mind seeing the report, too." She leaned across the table and fed him a spoonful of chocolate. "I realize I don't know your particular business, but I might be able to offer some advice from a consumer's point of view."

He accepted another bite, at the same time noticing how nicely her breasts were being pushed up as she fed him. "I'll send you a copy, if you're serious."

"I'm serious." She scooped out the last bit, closed her eyes as she swallowed it, then licked the spoon.

He watched her mouth. "I have never seen anyone enjoy chocolate like you."

"I like whipped cream, too." She batted her eyes and smiled.

He laughed. "Sounds cold."

"You've never tried it?"

"Nope. Why, have you?"

"Well, no. But I've always wanted to."

"On our weddin' night, then."

She lost her playfulness instantly. ''You promised, Lucas.''

''It wasn't the *M* word. It was the *W* word. And you were teasin' me, darlin'. I just had to tease back.'' He stretched out his leg, automatically doing the exercises he was supposed to do several times a day. It'd been a long day, though, and his knee was sore. ''We should probably head back to your place. I've got to get to the airport by eleven.''

''You do? But— I figured you'd spend the night. Can't you? You could fly back early in the morning.''

A discreet tap on the door delayed his reply. The waiter entered and asked if they needed anything else.

''Nothing, thanks,'' Luke said. ''We'll just leave when we're ready.''

''Very good, sir.'' The waiter removed the dessert goblets, then shut the door with a quiet click.

''I brought a hired pilot with me, Ariel. I wanted to work on the way. He's waitin' at the airport.''

''So, put him up in a hotel.''

''I can't.'' He took hold of her hand as she fiddled with her waterglass. ''His wife is expectin'. I promised him he'd be home in time to sleep beside her.''

Ariel looked away. A part of her wanted to beg. The long-independent, totally self-sufficient woman cut off the words before they spilled out. She wished she was pregnant and visibly in need for him to sleep beside—

She swallowed. Where had that image come from? Needing to stop thinking about it, she stood. ''Let's go, then.''

Twenty minutes later they stood in her entry as he helped her out of her coat. She reached for it and hung it in the closet.

''Thank you for tonight, Lucas. It was a nice surprise and a lovely evening.'' She walked back to him, trying to stay cheerful.

''What's wrong with you, Ariel?''

''Wrong?''

''C'mere.'' He put his arms around her and pulled her

close, until she leaned comfortably against him, her arms locked around his waist, his chin resting on her head. "I'm the last person you need to hide anything from."

Ariel squeezed her eyes shut. She was just so tired. The nightmares had come back, worse than ever. Every time the phone rang or someone knocked, she jumped, expecting some reporter. Every time she was in her car, she watched her rearview mirror almost more than the road. She couldn't live like this much longer.

She didn't want to go into analysis again. She'd had years of it as a child. If she just had one night with Luke. One night to make love, then sleep undisturbed. If she married him—

No. What a stupid reason to marry someone.

"Tell me, Ariel. Let me help."

"I need you, Lucas."

Luke tightened his hold. He'd done a damn good job of fighting his attraction all night. He'd wanted them just to have a date, a normal date like millions of other couples had every night. It was too much to hope, he supposed. They didn't have a normal relationship.

He leaned back to look at her face. Such a pretty face it was. And such a tired-looking one. He stroked her cheek with his fingers, ran his thumb across her lips. "I seem to need you, too," he said, giving up the fight. "I didn't want sex to be so important. I just wanted us to get to know each other—"

"Shh." She patted his chest with hands that wouldn't stay still. Her fingers fidgeted with his tie. "I want you so much. I can't tell you how much."

His mouth descended on hers like a bird of prey swooping down for the kill. Her head tipped back as he attacked her mouth with a restrained sort of violence that he hadn't shown her before and that she welcomed.

"Don't hold back this time," she whispered as he angled his mouth the other direction. "Don't hold me back, either."

"No." He kissed her hard. "Not this time." He tugged

on her lower lip with his teeth, swept his tongue into her mouth, pulled on her hair to tip her head back farther so that he could slide his open mouth down her throat. He dipped his tongue into her cleavage.

Ariel arched back and groaned. When he lifted his head, she saw need glitter in his eyes. Need for her. Deliberately, she loosened his tie, pulled it slowly from under his collar and tossed it aside. His gaze never left hers as she undid each of his shirt buttons, tugging the tail free and shoving the garment down and off him. She hooked a hand under his waistband. He stopped her.

"In the bedroom," he said gruffly. "I wish I could carry you. I want to carry you in there and drop you on the bed and cover your body with mine," he continued as he slid his hands over her rear and pulled her hips against his. "My knee won't support—"

She put her hand on his mouth, stopping his words. "I don't need gestures. Just honesty." She slipped a hand between them and shrouded his hard male heat. "This is honest. So is the look in your eyes. The time we shared at the cabin was wonderful, and I needed your tenderness then."

"And now?"

"Now I just need."

Somehow they made it to the bedroom. She turned on the tiny lamp by her bed, then she faced him, watching as he swept the bed covers back. He'd already kicked off his shoes. He started to unbuckle his belt.

"May I?" she asked.

He held his hands out in answer, giving her permission. But first she ran her fingers through the hair covering his chest. She touched the tip of her tongue to each nipple. He cupped the back of her head and held her as she explored him, loving his reaction as she followed the line down his stomach with her lips while she unbuckled his belt.

"I used to hate hairy chests." She tugged down his zipper, the sound an aphrodisiac of anticipation.

"Why?"

"I don't know. I love yours."

He sucked in a breath as she pushed his clothes to the floor. He stepped out of them, bending to pull off his socks as well. Then he stood before her, and she sighed.

"I can touch this time, right?" she asked.

"Yeah." He jerked back when she did. "Your hands are like ice."

"And you're so hot, Lucas. So scorchingly hot." She surrounded his hardness with her hands, traced intriguing veins with her fingertips, admiring him openly, blatantly. She tossed her hair back with an abrupt move as she needed to see his face. All of him was hard, from his furrowed brow all the way down to his feet planted solidly on the floor.

He hooked her dress with his hands and pulled. "I've been wanting to do this all night."

Cool air bathed her skin as he peeled the gown down her, inch by inch.

"I've been imaginin' you stark naked under this. You would've enjoyed some of the fantasies that have kept me wantin' you all night."

"I've been having my own."

"I noticed."

The dress pooled at her feet. He covered her breasts with his hands, let the weight of them rest in his palms, then teased the taut crests with his fingers until she dropped her head back and called his name.

"I'd forgotten how beautiful you are," he said, sitting her on the bed to remove her shoes and stockings. "I'm tempted to leave these on. But I don't want anything between us."

"Good," she breathed, welcoming his mouth against hers. She felt the mattress dip with the weight of his knee. "Lie down," she said. "It's my turn."

She took her time getting to know him, lingering when she knew she was driving him wild. She hadn't realized the power of lovemaking, how exciting it was to lead, to keep control of the moment, to take him up to the peak, then to back off at the last second. Full of newly found confidence, she knelt over him, letting her mouth go where her hands had explored, aroused by the textures of his body, so different from hers. Oh, the pleasure of loving him, of hearing him call her name, harsh and low, of watching his muscles become more and more defined as his body grew taut everywhere. The beauty of his maleness staggered her, the heat of it warmed her mouth when she dared to touch, to taste. To enjoy. To love.

With a harsh cry and a violent movement, he grabbed her shoulders and pushed her flat.

"Enough, temptress. I can't stand another minute of your torment."

His eyes were dark, hard, glittering. She'd done that. She. With a smile she hoped was sultry, she stretched her arms above her head and arched her back, offering her breasts.

"And to think I thought you were wholesome," he muttered, moving his hand over her body in one continuous stroke.

She purred.

He sucked a nipple into his mouth, pulling her higher in reaction as his hand slid low to cup her.

"You're so hot," Luke whispered as he tongued her nipple. "And wet. Anxious, darlin'?"

"Desperate."

"Ahh. Good. Then you know exactly how I feel."

"How do you feel?"

She tipped her pelvis a little, an invitation he didn't resist. "Like I've never felt before," he said, nudging her legs farther apart, letting his fingers seek the intimacy she begged for silently. He stroked and stopped, teased and stopped, swirled and stopped. He lost count of the number of times she climaxed. One ran into another. He was in danger of losing control just watching and listening to her.

"Enough, Lucas. Enough," she panted. "I can't stand it."

He moved over her body and entered her, then lay perfectly still, not wanting the end to come yet.

"I want to be on top," she whispered. "Can I be on top?"

They rolled together, mouths joined, bodies joined. She rose up and straddled him, and all he could see was Ariel as she rode him, her hair wildly tossed, her eyes intense. She told him how he felt inside her, how he filled her up, how she could remember the warmth of him in the shower at the cabin when he spilled into her, how she couldn't wait to feel it again.

His body was long past ready but his mind fought reaching the end. He wanted it to last forever. To listen to her forever. He'd fantasized that sex could be like this—hot, wild, open—but reality had never come close before. There was nothing shy in her actions, nothing coy in her words.

It wouldn't be enough. He'd want her again during the night. And again. And again. He didn't want to leave her.

"Ariel."

He knew how his voice must sound—desperate, maybe even angry.

"Let it happen, Lucas."

He lost control. He could hear his own voice fill the room. He drove up and up as she leaned her hands against his chest for balance. It wasn't ever going to stop. It just kept coming and coming, in waves of pleasure so strong he was paralyzed by it. Finally, it slowed…faded…

He pulled her down, wrapped her tightly in his arms and held her. She nestled against him. He could feel her contentment. He'd just ruined everything.

Sex with her wasn't supposed to be so all-consuming. It was going to get in the way all the time now. It was bound to change everything between them. All he would think about was how much he wanted her. No other woman had done the things, said the things, she had. He was getting hard again just thinking about the huskiness of her voice when she told him how good he felt as she squeezed him, locking him inside her. He wanted to immerse himself in the sights and scents and sounds once more. Now.

"Again?" Ariel asked sleepily. Against her abdomen, she felt him growing hard.

"I wish I had time." He kissed her forehead. "I've got to get to the plane, though."

"I wish you could stay. But I know you can't," she added quickly. She felt much more sure of their relationship now. She'd been worried that at the cabin, he'd made love to her as a kind of therapy. What happened tonight wasn't therapy. He'd wanted her. Needed her.

He tucked the blankets around her as he climbed out of bed. It took him a few minutes to gather his clothes and get dressed. He finally sat beside her on the bed. "I'll stay with you until you fall asleep," he said, stroking her forehead.

Ariel marveled at his self-control. Marveled at and admired and hated it. "Don't I get a kiss good-night?"

It was the sweetest kiss he'd ever given her, a gentle merging of lips that for some odd reason was more arousing than any of the more blatantly sexual kisses they'd shared. Something else was connected to this soft, lovely kiss, something beyond physical need.

How had he known she needed his gentleness right then?

"Close your eyes, now, darlin'."

He continued to stroke her forehead until she could feel herself floating, drifting, flying. Flying?

She opened her eyes. "You'll call me when you get home, won't you?"

"Shh. Of course I will. Quiet, now."

"Okay." She yawned. "Okay."

The phone rang. She grabbed it blindly. "H'lo."

"Home safe."

She blinked a few times. "Lucas? You were just here."

He chuckled, low and soft, the sound tugging at her insides.

"I left a couple of hours ago. You drifted right off."

"I must have."

"See how handy I'd be if you had me around all the time? Night, darlin'."

"G'night." She hung up the phone and snuggled under the covers again. Hey! He'd done it again. Mentioned the *M* word without using the *M* word. Damn the man, anyway, she thought, but with less heat than before.

She dragged Posse into her arms, using the stuffed dog to warm her chest. Something fell against her hand. She jumped, startled.

She turned on the lamp and shook the covers. A bead-and-feather-decorated woven circle tumbled free of the blankets. Luke must have put it there after she fell asleep.

She picked up the phone and dialed his number.

"You can't yell at me," he said instead of hello. "I didn't use the *M* word."

"You're too clever, Lucas, but I didn't call to yell. I wanted to say thank you."

"For what?"

"The dream catcher." She could almost hear him settle back, almost hear him smile.

"Did it work?"

In the beginning she'd thought him uncomplicated. She'd never expected he had the potential to surprise her, but he did—constantly. "Yes, it worked. Lucas, I have to tell you—I've never known anyone like you."

"Is that good?"

She smiled. "That's good."

"Okay. Ariel? We've got some issues to work out."

"I know."

"After my presentation next week. We can't put it off forever."

"Can't we just continue on—"

"No, darlin'. We can't."

She sighed. "You can be a real bulldozer when you want to be, Mr. Walker."

"Success doesn't come from stickin' your head in the sand, no matter how attractive you look bent over with your *be*hind stickin' up in the air."

She laughed, soft and sleepy. "Personally, that's not the angle I'd prefer anyone looking at."

"I can't imagine ever gettin' tired of the view, myself. 'Night."

Twelve

Ariel stepped out of her Explorer into the crisp Nevada morning. She stretched out the kinks from the long drive while she admired the view of the snow-dusted Sierra Nevadas, then she turned around and looked at the Titan building, debating whether to go inside. Today was Luke's big meeting. She was here to lend moral support. The only problem was, she didn't know if he wanted her here.

She was trying very hard to blame his meeting today as the cause of his distraction this past week, but she didn't know that for sure. He'd been distant with her since they'd made love. Whenever she mentioned it, he'd either clam up or change the subject.

She flipped her hair over the shoulders with a quick movement. She had enough confidence in their relationship to believe it was the pressure of the board meeting. She did. She believed that.

If you're so confident, why are you standing out here in the parking lot freezing your buns off? she asked herself.

Ariel trudged through the parking lot, then announced herself to the receptionist in the lobby. After a minute Marguerite appeared.

"Is Luke expecting you?" she asked.

"No. I know he's got the big meeting. I'll just say a quick hi, then I'll find something to do until he's done. I haven't played the one-armed bandits in a long time. Maybe I'll hit the casinos, then come back later. I just thought he'd like to know I'm around."

The two women wove through the maze of hallways of the corporate headquarters. Luke had talked of relocating to a metropolitan area, then decided against it. Although it was off the beaten path, the staff loved living there. Plus they were close enough to major cities. It wasn't a total inconvenience, except maybe during blizzards.

Marguerite knocked on Luke's door, then opened it a crack. "You've got company."

"Unless it's—"

"It's Ariel."

"You're kidding."

Ariel pushed the door open. "Surprise." She walked around Marguerite and into the room. "I know you're busy. I just came to wish you luck and invite you to dinner to celebrate tonight."

The door closed behind her. Luke stood in the middle of the room, a piece of paper in his hand, his jacket off, tie loosened, shirt cuffs rolled up, looking every inch the businessman. Nearby stood some easels holding visual aids—charts and graphs.

He hadn't said anything to her, just stared at her as if she were an apparition. Finally he crumpled the paper into his fist and tossed it into a trash can.

She took a step back. "Obviously I made a mistake. I'm sorry. I won't bother you any—"

"No. Ariel, wait. You surprised me, that's all. I'm glad to see you."

"Well, I won't keep you. I'm going to go lose some money at the slot machines and leave you to your work."

"Stay awhile. I can take a break." He finally really focused on her. "I've got some fresh tea here. Want some?"

She nodded, confused. Too much had happened in the past month. She didn't feel like herself anymore. Three weeks had gone by since their photograph appeared in the newspaper, and nothing seemed to have come of it. For the first time since then, she'd relaxed. Even sleep came easier these days. But now she didn't know what to think.

Luke handed her a mug and invited her to sit on the sofa with him. "Are you feeling okay?" he asked when they settled.

"I'm fine." He was looking so intently at her that it worried her. That and the fact he hadn't kissed her hello. "Look, I'm obviously in the way here."

He wrapped a hand around her wrist. "No, you're not. Are you sure you're okay?"

She frowned. "Yes, I'm sure. Why?"

"You still look tired."

"I look the same as always." This was not the time to get into a debate with him, she decided. He should be relaxed, confident, professional. Tired of waiting for him to kiss her, she leaned over and kissed him. He cupped her head, holding her still as he kissed her back, hard and quick, then he released her.

She sat back, blinking at the speed and intensity of the gesture. "Um, on that note, let's start over, shall we? Hello, Mr. Walker. How are you today?"

He smiled. "I'm fine, Miz Minx, thank you. And how are you?"

"*Very* well, thanks." She reached into her pocket and pulled out a richly polished wooden tube, about eight inches long. "I'm dying to know why you sent me a cigar."

"Well, now, that's not just a cigar. It's a symbol."

She eyed the tube. "A symbol? The obvious one?"

He laughed. "No. That, my dear Miz-I-Hate-the-Stinkof-Those-Blasted-Things, is the last cigar I'm gonna smoke.''

''Seriously?''

''I realized I've been smokin' too much since I quit football. What started as a relaxing kind of pretension turned into something else. I'm givin' it up. 'Course, I kinda figured I'd have a few more days to enjoy my addiction.''

She tucked it back in her pocket. ''I'll save it for the weekend, if you want—as long as I'm not breaking any laws by hanging on to it. I assume you would save your best *Cuban* cigar for your last.''

''You don't need to fret about the cops takin' you in. It's Cuban, all right, and just about the most expensive little roll of tobacco on this earth. But it's only illegal to bring them into the country, not to possess 'em.''

The intercom buzzed. ''Yes, Marguerite?''

''Sorry, Luke, but you told me to buzz you when the whole team was in the conference room.''

''I'll be there in a minute.'' He cut the connection and turned to Ariel. ''Don't go. I've got to attend a staff meeting, then I'll be back. Make yourself at home.''

''Okay.''

When he reached the door, he stopped, his hand on the knob, and looked back at her a second.

She watched him go, only the slightest hitch in his gait. She pressed a hand to her stomach as confusion and tension warred within her. Why had he looked so serious? What had changed in the past week?

More important, when had she fallen in love with him? She blew out a breath as the realization settled. It had happened so gradually she wasn't even aware of it until she walked through his office door and saw him standing there. She knew right then there wasn't anyplace else on earth she'd rather be than with him.

She should have known by the fact she'd revealed more to him every time they talked, trusted him more, cared about him more with every passing day. He made her laugh. She felt safe with him. She could cry with him, too. She'd never been able to do that with anyone before. Not anyone.

It had to be love.

But did that complicate their lives or make it easier?

Hoping he'd invite her to spend the night, she decided to arrange for someone to take over her meal deliveries tomorrow. She sat in Luke's big leather chair behind his desk, dialed a number and leaned her head against the chair back, smiling. Everything in the room smelled like him. Oh, she was a goner, all right.

"Claire? Hi, it's Ariel. Can you cover for me tomorrow? I'll take Saturday for you."

"Sorry, Ariel, I can't. Morgan could, I'll bet."

"I don't have his number with me. Do you have it?"

"Sure, just a sec."

Ariel picked up a pen, then looked for a scratch pad. Not seeing one, she opened Luke's top drawer. Her gaze landed on a piece of paper, mostly typed, but with a penciled notation toward the bottom—her name.

"Here's Morgan's number, Ariel."

On the desk blotter, Ariel wrote down the number without conscious thought, muttered her thanks, then hung up the phone with precise care as she pulled the clipped stack of papers out of the drawer and dropped it on the desk as if it were poisonous.

The heading consisted of one word: Wife. Below it was a list of names. Eight typed names, each with a line drawn through it, then her name in pencil, followed by the words: professional do-gooder. She winced. She lifted the top page, finding a report from the private investigation firm of Jerry Meyer, then another and another and another. One for each name on the list. Finally, at the bottom, hers.

Oh, God. She was going to be sick. The names were listed like candidates for a job. How could he have done that? How could he? Was she just part of a master plan? Would he have offered a salary, provided a retirement income and benefits?

This explained the diamond ring, too. One ring fits all. It

didn't matter which woman got it. They were interchangeable.

She stared at the list of crossed-off names, recognizing some—Cassie, Judith, Madeline—wasn't she the woman who'd bid for his jersey? Shannon—his *doctor?* A famous Hollywood actress. He knew *her?*

Had all the others rejected him and he'd turned to Ariel as his last resort? He must have seen how easily she could be swayed by his charm. It'd worked, too. She'd fallen in love with him.

She'd been kidding herself all along. Destiny couldn't be changed. She was stupid to have ever thought otherwise.

Luke left the conference room. Everything was in place. Everyone knew their roles. It had taken years to reach this point, but he'd earned it, fair and square.

First, however, there was Ariel. He wondered how she would take the news he'd gotten just as she arrived. He'd given up anticipating her reaction because she continually surprised him. Not that he was going to tell her right now. No, he'd save it for later, when they wouldn't be interrupted, when they could calmly and rationally discuss the situation.

He strode into his office, finding it empty except for Marguerite, who stood behind his desk, some papers clutched in her hand, her face white.

"What's wrong?" He looked around. "Where's Ariel?"

"She's gone."

"Gone? What do you mean, gone?" He looked again, expecting to see her pop out from behind the door and yell, "Surprise!"

Marguerite held out the papers. "These were on your desk. I don't remember seeing them there this morning."

Luke walked slowly forward. He knew the contents of the papers without looking. "Damn it. *Damn* it. How did she…" He shoved his fingers through his hair.

"Find them? I don't know. I told you what a dumb idea that was. I told you."

"Yeah. You told me." He shut down inside. He swore even his heart stopped beating. "I blew it." He searched the room blindly, as if some magical creature would take over for him, make the decisions, set everything in motion. "I have to go after her."

"You can't. This is the most important meeting of your life. The board's looking for any reason to question your having been made president. You have to see it through."

"Ariel—"

"Will have to wait." Marguerite slammed the papers on the desk. "We're all depending on you, Luke. We're all behind you. If you're not given a new contract, this company's going to sink, and all of us with it."

He moved to the window and searched the parking lot. No sign of her car. She could have been gone as long as half an hour. He probably couldn't catch her. And if he did, what could he say to her?

He thought of her driving the mountain roads, angry and humiliated. He thought of her crying. Or maybe she wouldn't. Maybe the anger would prevent that. He couldn't blame her. He'd messed up everything. Everything. Would she forgive him? Would she believe him when he told her the truth?

Ariel Minx was an all-or-nothing kind of woman.

And just when he'd been on the verge of having it all, he now faced having nothing.

Ariel watched her speedometer closely and eyed the road carefully. She wasn't going to let her anger make her careless and end up hurting herself or some innocent bystander. Every time thoughts of Luke trespassed on her thoughts, she turned up the radio and sang. She'd been hurt before. She would recover, be stronger than ever, just like before. From now on she'd trust her instincts more.

She parked in front of her apartment, intending to leave as soon as she threw a few things in a suitcase and made arrangements for someone to take over her duties for a while.

She didn't have any idea where she was going. South, probably. Someplace warmer. San Diego, maybe. That was about as far south as she could get in California.

The wooden stairs leading to her apartment creaked. She concentrated on the noise and on her feet, so she didn't see the man sitting at the top until she almost tripped on him.

"Go home, Lucas. You are the last person I want to see right now."

"I need to—"

"How did you beat me here?" she interrupted. "Oops. Dumb question to ask a man with his own personal jet, huh?"

He looked terrible. She couldn't muster an ounce of sympathy for him.

"Ariel—"

"What are you doing here, anyway? You've got your big meeting," she said, proud of her coolness.

"We need to talk."

"Oh, I don't think so, Lucas. I really don't think so." She moved past him and shoved her key in the lock. "Your *charmin'* talk is what got me into this mess in the first place."

"I know you're angry. You have every right to be angry."

"Thank you so much."

"All I'm asking for is a few minutes to explain. Won't you give me that much?"

She didn't want to give him the satisfaction of knowing just how much she was hurting, so she invited him in. She settled into an overstuffed chair, leaving him either to stand or to sit on the couch. She didn't care what he did.

The apartment was cold. Luke adjusted the thermostat, giving himself something to do, trying not to think about everyone at Titan who was waiting for him. The most important person at the moment sat primly across from him.

"Oh, before you start," Ariel said with utter nonchalance. "Here." She tossed him the wooden cigar holder.

He hefted it, frowned, then looked inside. "This is empty."

"I gave it to someone who would appreciate it more."

"Who?"

"I don't know his name. He lives in a cardboard box a few blocks over. He thanks you with all his heart. Said he's never had a whole cigar before."

"Not just any cigar. That was an Arturo Fuente Opus X."

"He hadn't heard of the brand, but I assured him it was prime stuff."

Luke clamped his mouth shut, stopping the potential argument. It was a cigar, after all. Just a stupid cigar. Although it seemed especially symbolic at the moment—close, but no cigar.

After a minute he started pacing as he argued his case. "Some people say I've led a charmed life, that everything came easy to me. What most people haven't seen—because I haven't let them—is how hard I've worked for everything I've gotten. Maybe because of the publicity manufactured for me, or maybe because I don't share my feelings easily I made it look easy. I probably don't seem intense to most people. But I'm driven to succeed. It's almost a sickness with me. I set a goal, then I do whatever it takes to accomplish it."

"Including finding a wife."

He sat on the couch and leaned forward. "I'd just given up football, Ariel. Not only the game, but the physical activity and, yes, even the status that went with it. It's not an easy transition, no matter how much I've told people otherwise. It was the hardest thing I'd done."

"I know that, Lucas. I do know that. I could see it."

"I believe you. And because of that, I relaxed with you. I did let you see when I was hurtin'. I let you in like no one ever in my life. I trusted you."

"And I'd come to trust you. Look where it got me. I was a name on a list. Interchangeable with any of the others." Her jaw clenched. "And that's another thing. Damn it, Lucas, I was penciled in. An afterthought! How come I was last on the list?''

''Truthfully? I don't know. You'd made it clear on the cruise you weren't interested in me. If you hadn't come to my office that day, I probably would've been workin' my way down the original list, and still been no closer to marryin' anyone.''

She snorted. ''Right. You'd already exhausted those possibilities. I saw the names crossed out. I thought you were going to be honest.''

''I am.'' He shoved his hands through his hair. ''Let me start at the beginnin'. I decided if I was gonna leave everything behind and start a new part of my life, I wanted to go all the way with it. I realized it was time to settle down.'' He watched her closely, gauging whether she was listening with an open mind or not. ''I put together a list of the single women I knew who might—might—be possibilities. Can't say it was one of my better ideas. They were just names, nothing more.

''Then you showed up. Everything changed. I never once took any of those women out in the hopes of marriage.''

''Is that true?''

''Why would I lie to you? After I saw you again, I put the list aside. A couple of days ago I was doodling on the paper while I was talkin' to you on the phone. I crossed out the other names. Felt really good, too. I meant to dump the whole packet in the shredder.''

''But what about the private investigator's reports?''

''I forgot I'd ordered them. I wanted some basic information, that's all. I couldn't afford to make any mistakes. It wasn't a good move, all right? I admit it, but I never even read the reports when they came in. They didn't mean anything to me anymore.''

''Including mine?''

He straightened. ''Yours? I didn't order one on you.''

''I saw it.''

''I swear to you that I didn't request one. I learned a few

pertinent facts from the report done on the Center. I told you what I learned. I didn't ask for anything else."

"Then how do you explain the report in your possession? Chase told me someone was snooping around, asking questions about me. I called you and asked who your P.I. was and you said Jerry Meyer. That's the name on my report."

"You asked about some other guy—"

"Douglas Jett."

"Well?"

"I *saw* the report."

"Was there something on there you didn't want me to see?"

"That's not the point."

He stood. "Come with me."

"Where?"

"To the kitchen. You have a speaker phone in there."

She didn't budge.

"I'm guilty of some things, Ariel, but not of violating your trust. Let me prove that much to you."

She followed him, already much calmer, although not willing to let him off the hook completely. She was ninth on his list! An alternate. Hardly even memorable.

Ninth, ha! He might regain her trust easily enough but her ego had suffered a big blow, she thought.

"Jerry, it's Luke Walker," he said when the investigator came on the line. "I hope you don't mind bein' on the speaker. I've got my hands full."

"No problem. What's up?"

"I've been goin' through those reports you put together for me—"

"Pretty interesting reading material, huh? Good thing you were smart enough to check those ladies out. I mean, you could've gotten hooked up with a couple of les—"

"Jerry," Luke interrupted. "I'm really pressed for time here. I want to know why I got a report on Ariel Minx."

"Oh, that was Doug's doing."

Luke sought Ariel's gaze. "Who's Doug and why did he do it?"

"I've got a new associate. He helped do the background you asked for on the youth center. Seems he got real interested in your Ms. Minx, particularly after seeing the newspaper photo of the two of you. Took it upon himself to make a few more inquiries. He asked me about it. I figured since you were checking out the rest of the women, it'd be okay. Did we screw up?"

"From now on, just do what I ask, okay, Jer? If you've got something else in mind, check with me first."

"You don't understand the investigator's mind, Luke. We like to dig, especially when someone's a puzzle, like Ms. Minx. Usually by the time we get done checking someone out, you wouldn't hire *or* date 'em. 'Course, the lady in question turned out to be an exception. Clean as a whistle. Too good for you, pal."

Luke hung up after saying goodbye. He leaned against the kitchen counter.

"Maybe I did overreact," Ariel said primly, defensively. Involuntarily she moved closer to him. "I've been overtired, and you've been acting weird all week."

"You had every reason to react the way you did. I'm sorry you were hurt. I wish you'd stayed and confronted me about it." He squeezed her shoulders. "You can't begin to imagine the hell I went through thinkin' about you drivin' through the mountains when you were spittin' mad. I was goin' out of my mind, worryin'." He stopped and drew a breath. "Don't ever do that to me again, angel. Just stay. Yell. Punch me in the stomach. Whatever. But don't run." He lifted her chin. "So, are we okay now?"

Angel. He'd called her angel. She wanted to cry. It was just suddenly all too much.

"Need a hug?" he asked so tenderly she did burst into tears.

He took her into his embrace, soothing her as she apologized profusely for being so emotional.

"I don't understand," she wailed. "I never cried until I met you."

"There might be a real good reason for that, darlin', and we'll need to talk about it, and some other things, as well. But for now I've got to get back. A whole lot of people are countin' on me."

She squeezed him a little tighter, then leaned back to look him in the eye. She took a deep breath. "Take me with you."

He frowned. "I can't. I have to get back right away. I flew—"

"I know that. Take me with you on your plane."

"Ariel," he breathed. "Are you sure?"

She wiped the tears from her face. "You said that the only way to overcome my fear was to challenge it. That I couldn't conquer it otherwise. I'm tired of that fear controlling me. I hate the way it turns me into a scared little girl. I'm all grown up. I need to prove it to myself before I can go on with the rest of my life. I thought I knew where I was headed. I don't think I'll really know until I've conquered my fear of getting in a plane again. And I trust you more than anyone, Lucas."

He brushed her hair with his fingers. "I don't know what to say. I'm humbled."

"Say you'll take me with you."

Thirteen

Luke watched her explore the cabin of the jet. They hadn't taken off yet and already she was shaking—and trying so hard not to show it.

"Are you sure?" he asked as she peeked into the bedroom. "If you're not comfortable with my pilot flyin' the plane, I can take over, and you can sit up in the cockpit with me."

"No." Her smile was but a flicker of movement. "This is better. You won't be distracted as much, in case I, well, panic or something."

"All right." He grabbed a blanket from the bed. "Let's bundle you up. You look cold. And we both need to buckle in."

She accepted the blanket he wrapped around her and followed docilely to the center cabin. The seats there were luxurious and spacious, with plenty of room for her and the blanket.

Not waiting for her to fumble with the seat belt, he buckled it himself, then sat beside her. "All set?"

She nodded. He buzzed the pilot. The plane started moving. Her fingers dug into the armrests; she squeezed her eyes shut.

He talked her through the first few minutes of the short flight. The takeoff was smooth, the ascent slow and steady. They'd had a little turbulence on the way to San Francisco earlier. He hoped they wouldn't run into much going back.

"You can open your eyes, darlin'. Nothin's going to change because you're not watchin'. In fact, with your eyes closed, you feel the plane's every little flutter. You'll do better if you're lookin' around instead."

Her eyes came open slowly. They were as dark as he'd ever seen them.

"Lucas?"

"What?"

"I think this would be an excellent time to be initiated into the mile-high club."

He smiled. "Do you, now? And how do you know about that elite group?"

"Oh, from here and there. That's a really nice bed you've got in the back. I wouldn't mind spending the time doing something constructive."

"So now sex is just constructive?"

"No, but— Oh, you know what I mean."

"You want oblivion."

As she nodded, he pushed up the armrest between them and put his arm around her, drawing her close. She rested her head against his chest, and he stroked her hair in long sweeps down her back.

"Why don't you just talk to me, instead, angel."

"About what?"

"You decide. Just start talkin'. I'll listen."

She didn't say anything for a while, then finally, "There were 167 passengers on the plane. I was the only survivor."

The unexpected words hit Luke like a two-by-four in the stomach. ‘‘What happened?’’

‘‘I told you the plane broke into pieces, that several of the back rows were ejected. My mother and I were together in the last row because she was pregnant and still got sick a lot. She needed to be near the rest rooms. The rest of my family were farther up. They died in the fire. Impact killed most everyone, anyway. They figure almost everyone suffered a broken neck.’’

‘‘Including your mother?’’

‘‘Yes.’’

‘‘Ariel.’’ He said her name in wonder. In comfort. In gratitude.

‘‘That's not my name. It's Angela. Angela Mazursky. That's why my family called me Angel.’’ Her fingers dug into his side. ‘‘I had to change my name. Change my identity. They wouldn't leave me alone.’’

‘‘Who wouldn't?’’

‘‘Reporters. Everyone called me The Miracle Child. The media was relentless. I was barely comprehending what had happened myself, and they wouldn't leave me alone, not for a second. You wouldn't believe the tricks some of them pulled to try to get to me. Anything for a quote.

‘‘My God, I was eight years old. I'd survived a plane crash that killed my whole family. I spent hours after the crash buckled into my seat, in the rain. It was so cold and so lonely. And my mother sat lifeless in the seat beside me, not answering me. Not hearing me. Not being my mother anymore. I was scared. I was just so scared. There was nothing I could do. And afterward, all I wanted to do was forget it.’’

Her experience was beyond his imagination. He didn't know what to do. What to say. His eyes stung as he pictured her with no one to offer comfort, no one to say everything would be all right. It wouldn't be all right. Nothing would ever be all right again.

And he'd been worried about shutting the door on a

damned football career... No wonder she was so strong. No wonder—

"I didn't speak for three months after," she continued. "Every person with any possible connection to my family claimed me for their own, wanted to be my guardian—because everyone figured I'd have huge settlements from the airlines. I was in court having my fate decided when my father's sister, my Aunt Bonnie, showed up. She'd been on one of her meditation treks and hadn't been notified about the crash until the day before. I'd always loved her best. She came storming into the judge's chamber. Oh, I was so glad to see her! I called her name and ran to her, and she held me like no one had for so long."

She rested her chin on Luke's shoulder. "The judge awarded me to her because I obviously loved her and because she didn't have need of my settlement money, so he knew she was taking me in for good reasons. He told her she'd have to stay on with me in the family home, to keep my roots there. He thought another change would be too disruptive for me."

Luke felt her tension ease a little. Amazed that she could relive that experience with him and still stay in control, he made himself loosen his grip. "But you grew up in Europe, you said."

"Because the media wouldn't let us get on with our lives. Every time an anniversary came around, or financial settlements were made, or another plane crashed, they'd camp on our doorstep, demanding my reaction. They would even call out questions while I was playing in the school yard at recess. It was destroying my life, what there was of it."

"So that's why you avoid publicity."

"Avoid. Shun. Hide out. You have no idea how many newspaper articles were written about me. And magazine stories. Plus the television profiles based on nothing but minimal research and maximum speculation. I was like some kind of freak, Lucas. I had daily sessions with a psychiatrist just to get me to cope. Yes, I dread publicity. I live in fear of someone finding out who I am. It'll start all over again."

"Is there much of a chance someone could find out? You've changed your name. How many people know that?"

"When I was in college, I told my roommate after three years of our being best friends. She promised not to tell anyone. Then the next thing I knew, her boyfriend wanted to interview me for the school newspaper. When I turned him down, he wrote an article, anyway. He just didn't put my name in it. All of it speculation, just like before."

"What did you do?"

"After I went crazy? I couldn't do anything without making a public case of it, so I just moved out. And from then on, I had the lowest profile any Stanford student has probably ever had. I lived in fear, wondering who else he'd told. I'd already started my life over once. I didn't want to have to do it again." She sat up, pushing away from him. "Why can't people understand that when you've been through an experience like that, more than anything you need normalcy in your life? I needed routine, and friends I could count on, and all the things that everyone wants."

Luke looked past the adult woman to the child she'd been. "Of course you did," he said gently.

"But every time I thought I found it, something happened to shake it all up again and the memories flooded back, worse than ever. It isn't something you just *get over.* You live with it. Deal with it. And somehow make peace with it. Nobody knows what to say to me. I understand that. There's really nothing to say. So I don't talk about it, even with trusted friends like Chase, who I know wouldn't tell anyone else, because the last thing I want is sympathy."

"You just want someone to listen."

"Yes!"

He wasn't sure what he'd done to deserve such absolute trust as she'd just placed in him.

"I was so afraid someone would see the picture of us in the paper and track me down."

"But no one did?"

"Not so far."

"What if someone had? What if someone does?"

"If it were yesterday, I don't know. Today—"

She stopped. Confusion spread across her face, then something he couldn't define.

"Today I feel strong enough to face it," she said, finishing the sentence.

"What's different today?"

You're here—and I love you. Ariel hadn't known she could find such strength in loving him. She kept the words locked inside, however, knowing she needed to hear the words from him first—and at a time when he wasn't feeling any pity for her, as he must be now, as any human being with any amount of compassion would. "I'm feeling invincible. Don't ask me why. I've never felt like this before. Like I could do anything. Go anywhere. Face anyone."

"My warrior." He smiled, then leaned across the space between them to kiss her.

She clung to him, turning the kiss from tender to demanding. She pulled back a little, her emotions simmering, threatening to come to a quick, hard boil. "I want you, Lucas. *Need* you. And it's not oblivion I'm looking for anymore. I've hardly been aware we're flying."

She watched him swallow. She could see him struggle with what to do with her. Although he'd hung up his suit jacket, he was still dressed for his business meeting. And time was short. She saw him run all the possibilities through his mind.

Abruptly he unbuckled his seat belt and stood. "I need something to drink. Can I get you anything?"

She pressed her hands to her forehead and sighed. "Some water would be fine."

He opened the refrigerator and pulled out two bottles. "Tell me about the name you chose for yourself."

"My aunt's pet name for me was Minx, so that became my last name. I decided on Ariel when I was fifteen, after seeing a production of a Shakespeare play, *The Tempest.* Ariel—usually a male character, but played by a woman in this production—is a sprite who embodies lightness and illumination. She helps the character Prospero employ good magic against evil, and is eventually freed from the spell she's under because of her good deeds, or at least that's the way I interpreted it. It made everything clear to me. More important, it gave me something to hold on to."

"I don't follow how Ariel's predicament relates to you." He passed her a glass, then sat beside her again.

"Don't you see? I survived for a reason. It *is* like a spell. What I do is an obligation, a daily commitment. Someday I'll have done enough to compensate."

"That's why you started the Angel Foundation."

She waved a hand. "The settlement is blood money to me. I hated it at first. I wanted to give it all away. My aunt wouldn't let me take control of it until I was mature enough to deal with it rationally. I give myself a salary out of the interest, because it's a full-time job. And I've almost doubled the initial amount through investments. It does rule my life, but there's so much to do.

"I had a second chance, Lucas. I'm trying to let others have theirs. As long as I do that, I'm free. I've paid back."

"Maybe," he said slowly, taking her hand in his, "it isn't so much what you do for others that will free you from the guilt—survivor's guilt, right? Maybe you won't find freedom until you finally do a good deed for yourself."

She looked past him as she considered his words. Did he mean that by marrying him she would be doing something for herself? That by doing so, she'd be freed of the burden she'd carried for twenty years? Could that be true? Had she paid enough? Over his shoulder she could see clouds through the window, white and billowy. The plane bounced a little. She crushed his hand.

"It's all right. Just a little turbulence. Nothing to worry about." He glanced out the window. "We're headin' down.

Be landin' pretty soon. This has been a helluva day for you, hasn't it?''

''I can't tell you what it meant that you followed me home. But I feel so guilty. Your meeting—''

''You feel guilty? After all you've been through, *you* feel guilty?'' He shook his head. ''Well, don't fret. I don't believe there'll be repercussions. In fact, it may have worked out better. By havin' each department head present their own prospectus instead of me doin' the whole presentation, the board will see the departments as individuals. As people, not just names on a chart. I'll just charm the socks off 'em to wind it all up.''

''Pretty sure of yourself.''

''Well, now, if I've convinced *you,* then maybe I can fool the board.''

She cocked her head. ''What do you mean?''

''You know me better than anyone. If you can't see I'm scared spitless over the outcome, then I might be able to pull it off.'' His hands tightened around his glass. ''I'm not sure of myself, not completely, but I'm damn sure of my plans for Titan. I've come up with a plan I know will work, so that we won't be takin' on new business before we're ready to handle it, but so that we can grow fast enough to capitalize on the booming market.'' He squeezed her hand. ''Do you want to trade seats with me and look out the window while we land?''

She shook her head. ''Maybe next time.''

''I admire you, Ariel. More than I can say.''

A few minutes later they taxied to a hangar at a private airstrip. As soon as the engines were shut down, the pilot rushed into the cabin.

''My wife's in labor, Luke.''

''Go. I'll get someone to take care of things here.''

''Thanks.'' He took off.

Luke looked at his watch, then at Ariel.

''I don't like that speculative look, Lucas Walker. What's going on?''

"The mile-high club, you said?" He walked to the open hatch and looked outside, then he pressed a button. The door closed, sealing off the cabin. "And I recall something about *want* and *need?*"

Inside her body, a conga line formed, dancing and weaving throughout as she returned his heated gaze. "Your meeting..."

Her words trailed off as he meandered toward her, his gaze intensifying.

Luke wanted to help her forget. *He* wanted to forget. She wouldn't accept sympathy, so he decided to let her find the oblivion she was looking for, after all. He noted her clothes—a white undershirt topped by a flannel shirt, both tucked into blue jeans that must have been cut to her body alone. On her feet were thick-soled boots. He wondered how little he could get away with removing.

"To hell with my meeting. I have time." He moved forward. "If you've got the interest?"

"Stupid question. How much time?"

He snatched the water glass from her hand and thunked it on the counter. Water sloshed everywhere. "Enough."

"Ooh, I like a man who takes charge."

"Like hell you do."

"Well, this time I do."

"Come here, Miz Minx."

"Don't get too carried away, now." She looked around. "No one can see in, can they?"

She shrieked as he tossed her over his shoulder and carried her to the bedroom in the back cabin, then dumped her on the bed. He straddled her thighs, undid her jeans and tugged them past her knees. He reached for his belt buckle, then the zipper.

Excited by the new role he'd assumed, Ariel didn't hide her interest in his actions. She wound his tie around her hand and spun it behind him, out of the way. "You *are* in a hurry."

"I hope you're not in need of a whole lot of foreplay, darlin'."

"As a matter of fact—" she pulled him down "—I'm not."

She sucked in a breath as their flesh touched. He didn't give her a second to enjoy it before he kissed her, aggressively, thoroughly, memorably. She loved the feel of him pressed against her, hard and masculine, ready to take her to paradise. She reached down to guide him, felt him jerk in reaction to her touch, heard the words he whispered, encouraging her. Hampered by their clothing, their movements were limited—and wildly intoxicating.

"Ah, darlin', you feel so good." Their bodies merged, caught fire, then flared out of control. "So damn good."

"Oh! Already," she said, surprised at the building pleasure. They could do little more than rock against each other. She couldn't wrap her legs around him, so she tipped toward him more, seeking a tighter union. He thrust harder, deeper. She cried out. He called her name. Then only the sound of harsh breathing filled the room.

"Did we," she panted, "just have…what's commonly referred to as…a quickie?"

"We did." He kissed her leisurely, until she moaned, shifting anxiously under him. "Feelin' used, are you, darlin'?"

"Well used. Wonderfully used." She sighed. "Isn't it nice that we don't have to worry about birth control? I love the spontaneity. Each time we've made love has been different."

Luke went still. He'd forgotten. God, he'd forgotten. She was never going to forgive him. If it even mattered at this point—

He leaned across her and snagged a box of tissues. "We'd better get a move on."

He watched her slide her underwear up her body. The frothy bit of bright blue silk branded an image into his mind he wouldn't soon forget. He wanted her again. He wanted to strip off all her clothes and spend a week with her, with nothing between them. No secrets. No obligations. Just them, locked in his mountain cabin. Or stuck on some remote tropical island all by themselves where they could swim naked and stretch out on the sand and make love whenever they wanted. He'd never get his fill of her, no matter how much time they had.

She touched his arm. "What's wrong?"

"We have to talk." He knew he was being abrupt. And after all she'd just shared with him, he should be his most tender. He ached for the little girl who'd been through such trauma. He ached for the woman who lived with it every day. He didn't want to make a mistake, to do something that might mess up her life more.

He pulled her into his arms and held her tight, burying his face in her hair. He had to do everything right this time. There was no margin for error. The wrong word could—

"Lucas, you're scaring me."

"What I have to tell you can't be told fast. We need time." He kissed the top of her head. "After my meeting is over, okay?"

"I don't seem to have a choice."

He hoped that wasn't the case. He hoped she'd be free to make her own choices. More than anyone he knew, she deserved that much.

Fourteen

Ariel paced Luke's office. Back and forth, back and forth. She plopped onto the sofa for five minutes, got up again, walked back and forth. Back and forth.

She tried to tell herself she was just worried about how this would all turn out for him. He deserved the chance to take Titan into the twenty-first century. The board had to see that his vision was sound.

Her thoughts kept drifting back to the rest of the day. She wondered how long they would have maintained the status quo between them without the jolt they'd had. But how bewildering that just when everything was right for her finally, he seemed to be changing his mind about what he wanted.

She trusted him completely. Out of that trust had come a love so deep it was frightening, a love so strong she was willing to live in the spotlight with him. What she'd feared most hadn't happened. By telling him everything and getting him to understand what drove her, she hadn't found the reason to turn down his marriage proposal, but to accept it.

She'd expected the words on the plane after they'd made love. Words that not only hadn't come but didn't seem even on the verge of coming now.

How ironic that she had changed her mind at the same time that he had changed his. Apparently he was happy only having a relationship, just as she'd thought that was what *she'd* wanted.

Tears welled. And that was another thing. She was sick of all the tears lately, all the anxiety, all the insecurity. She couldn't even remember the last time she'd cried before Luke had come into her life. It was all his fault.

And it was wonderful. She felt so alive. Emotions bubbled in her, an unfamiliar but welcomed froth of feeling. She wasn't willing to give it all up without a fight.

She paced some more. He should follow through with what he started—that's all there was to it. He's the one who started her dreaming of having family and home and continuity. He's the one who proposed! She was perfectly happy with her life until then. Well, maybe not perfectly...

She sighed. She'd just been going through the motions until then. There hadn't been any highs or lows, just a pleasant routine—she refused to call it monotony—that she could count on day to day. If she had to go back to that now, she'd die.

She turned around when she heard someone coming into the room.

"Luke sent me," Marguerite said. "We're having a celebration in the conference room. He wants you to come."

"He got what he wanted?"

"A five-year commitment. But he's not the only one who won. We all did." They walked out of the office. "I guarantee he'll be trading *Sports Illustrated* covers for *Business Week.*"

Ariel ignored the automatic flutter in her stomach. After a minute the feeling faded. She was proud of him and happy for him.

In the conference room Luke hugged her, then he released

her right away to pour champagne as more employees drifted in and picked up glasses to be filled. The mood should have been contagious. Ariel not only felt out of place, but anxious. This would be the ideal time for Luke to introduce his bride-to-be to his employees. He didn't introduce her, period.

After a while she returned to his office. Night had settled like a dark question, matching her mood. She turned off all the lights and pulled his big desk chair up to the window. She swallowed the lump in her throat. Even if she'd wanted to run, she couldn't. She didn't have her car this time.

She swallowed again, around a more painful lump. She'd never let herself love anyone before. If she had to give him up, would the love just go away with time, or was there something she'd have to do to make it die?

A soft click alerted her the door was opening. A shaft of light from Marguerite's office spilled in, broken by Luke's shadow.

"Ariel?"

"Over here, by the window."

He came up beside her. "Why'd you leave?"

"I couldn't take the noise." Which was just a little lie, after all. She didn't think he realized he'd hurt her by not introducing her to everyone. "Congratulations. You got more than you hoped."

"Yeah. I'm pleased."

"So. Why don't you tell me what's been on your mind all day, Lucas."

Luke shut the door and turned on a couple of lights. He saw her boots lying jumbled on the floor beneath the chair. Her legs were tucked under her, her hands locked in her lap. He leaned against the window, the cold from the glass seeping into him. "I want to tell you how the list came about."

Her eyes flickered. "I'm not sure I want to hear this."

"We have to clear the air. Things can't go on like they were." When she crossed her arms, he began. "I told you about my engagements, what went wrong with them."

"You'd mistaken lust for love, you said."

"With all the changes in my life recently, I decided it was time to get married, as well, and find some way to have a family. I thought that this time around I was mature enough, with no excuses for makin' the same mistakes. I should do things differently. I figured I shouldn't choose a woman I wanted to sleep with, but one I could look across the breakfast table at without wishin' I could take her right back to bed. You know...a friend." It sounded even more ridiculous when he voiced it aloud, Luke realized. And the scowl that formed on her face confirmed it.

"You picked me because you *weren't* attracted to me?"

Hell. "Well...initially."

She pushed herself out of the chair and marched up to him. "I was all over you, and you didn't care? You don't find me desirable? Have you been faking it?"

"Now, hold on, Ariel. I was confused. I only knew things had to be different this time."

"You're not physically attracted to me?" she asked hoarsely.

He could see he couldn't get on with his confession until they'd dealt with this issue. "Sex had always been fun for me. Simple. Easy. Sex with you is the best of my entire life, and that's the truth. I'm tellin' you I was fightin' havin' it that way. I knew it would spoil things."

She blinked. He could see her sort through his words. "The best?" she repeated.

"Ever. I didn't want it to be. I still don't want it to be."

"Why not?"

"Because sex gets in the way of what's important. I wanted to have a mature relationship. I wanted us to be friends. I wanted you by my side while I grew my business. I wanted to be able to talk to you about anything."

"And I wanted *not* to be the perfect hostess, for once, and the volunteer everyone depends on," she countered. "I wanted a physical relationship. I got that. But I also found a lot more besides."

"You truly did just want my body?"

"I was afraid of you from the moment I met you, Lucas, and that's the truth."

"Afraid? I wouldn't ever lay a hand on you—"

"Not that kind of fear. I'd never felt that kind of attraction, and it scared me. I didn't know what to do with it, so I backed away from you. Then when we spent more time together, I accepted that it was stronger than my fear. But I figured you'd *want* a physical relationship. I thought most men would."

He scratched his head. "And here I was wantin' just the opposite for the first time in my life. My intentions were useless, anyway. The sex is great, Ariel. It's been great from the beginning. Seems like no matter what I did, how I tried to distract myself, I got carried away, even though I tried my damnedest not to let it take priority."

She stared at him a minute, her mouth agape, then she put a hand to her forehead and looked at the floor, shaking her head, muttering something under her breath.

"What?" he asked.

She looked up. She had the strangest expression on her face. Bafflement, humor, even some kind of hurt. "Do you know why, Lucas?"

"Why I tried to resist you? I told you. Because it'd screwed up every other relationship—"

"No. Do you know why it was the best sex ever?"

"Is this a test?"

She laughed. Then her eyes filled with tears so fast he couldn't figure where they came from. Hell. She hadn't cried when she relived the worst moment in her life, but she was crying now. What the hell did that mean?

"Yes, it's a test," she said, her voice catching.

"Multiple choice?" he asked hopefully.

"You nitwit." She laughed and cried at the same time. "The sex is the best ever because, A, you love me. B, you love me. C, you love me. Or D, all of the above."

"I do?" He swallowed. He stared at her silly smile and her watery eyes. Tension seeped out of him. His legs turned rubbery. He needed to sit down and absorb the moment of instant realization. He loved her. It wasn't just lust and friendship. Well, it was, but it was more. So much more. And completely definable. "I *do.* I love you."

"How's that for ruining your big plans?" she asked.

Meaning what? he wondered. She didn't return the feelings to the same degree? Of course she did. She seemed to be waiting for something, though. Maybe…

He moved her aside so that he could open his top desk drawer and pull out a small dark blue velvet box. She retreated as he opened the lid. "I believe I've found your purpose you've been looking for," he said, reaching for her, keeping her close.

"What?"

"I think you're here to love me, angel. What do you think?"

"Maybe."

"Maybe? Damn it, Ariel. You are. I know it. If this doesn't prove it, I don't know what does." He shoved the box her way.

Ariel stared at the ring there. It wasn't the diamond he'd offered before, but something else. Her hand hovered over it, shaking. She couldn't touch it.

"I've spent so many hours ponderin' you," he said in a voice rough with emotion. "Tryin' to figure you out was like tryin' to figure out what makes dogs howl at the moon. There's some scientific explanation for why they do it, but knowin' it doesn't change anything. You are who you are. There's no one else like you. And that's why I fell in love with you. Now, I admit when I first proposed marriage to you, I didn't know what I was really askin' of you. But now I do. I'm askin' you again to marry me, Ariel. And I figure you want to know why, so I'll tell you that, too. It's because you're like those orchids I sent, dainty and delicate, and long-lasting and sturdy. It's because you eat chocolate the same way you make love, as a sensual experience.

"It's because you care more about everyone else on earth

than yourself, and you need for someone to care more about *you* than anyone. I'm that man. I'm gonna love you until there's no breath in me to say the words. I'm gonna love you so hard you won't know a second of insecurity about it. I'm gonna love you whether you want me to or not, so you might as well just accept it. You're doomed to have me forever."

He pulled the ring out of the box and held it up.

"I must've looked at a hundred stones before I found the one that was you. It's called a fire opal, and if you look close you can see yourself deep inside."

Ariel couldn't see anything through her tears. She took his word for it.

"See, the surface catches your eye first. It's pale and pretty and it makes you look twice. Then you angle it just a little and you can see it sparkles underneath, and you find you can't stop lookin' at it. Then when you look way down inside, past the sparkles, you see the fire there. It's all lit up with passion and heat. It's you, Ariel. Only you. Always you. And I am gettin' really nervous because you haven't uttered a peep. So, please put me out of my misery and tell me you love me, too."

"I love you." She threw herself at him. "I love you."

"And you'll marry me?"

"Yes. Oh, yes."

"Well, that's a relief, 'cause I think you might be pregnant."

"What?" She took a few steps back.

"When you got here this morning, I'd just gotten a fax from my doctor. I had a fertility test done. I'm not sterile."

She flattened her hands on her abdomen. Hope flared. "I don't understand. Why didn't that—that *woman* get pregnant?"

"One of life's great mysteries. Maybe my count was low at the time. It's not overly high now, but I *am* fertile." He eased a little closer. "Or maybe your mother was watchin' from heaven and had already picked me out for you and somehow she intervened."

She smiled. "Oh, I like that. Yes. Maybe she did."

He slipped the ring on her finger, then turned her hand over and kissed her palm.

"Lucas." He was a man of gestures, she realized. Big gestures, little gestures. She would always know how much he loved her, because he would always show her in some way all his own. Oh, he really was the best man she knew. The very best. And with him she could do anything. Conquer any fear. Share her dreams. Love unconditionally. She stroked his hair. *Thanks, Mom. You made a wonderful choice for me.*

He straightened. "Do you think you might be?"

"Pregnant? No. Or I wasn't before today, at least. Maybe now, though."

"Would that be all right? I should've told you first thing this morning. I should've remembered before we made love unprotected. I'd like to say I just forgot, because basically I did. But I think a part of me wanted it to happen. If that makes me a chauvinist—"

She laughed. "You're not a chauvinist, Lucas. You're just you. I love you just the way you are." She wound her arms around his neck and pulled herself snugly against him. "I'd kind of like to have some time to enjoy the best sex anyone's ever had before I have a belly getting in the way. But we can let nature take its course, I suppose. Don't do anything to make it happen, or not make it happen. We still don't have any guarantees, you know. At least I know you'd be willing to adopt if *I* can't have children."

"Knowin' you, darlin', we'll probably have a houseful. Maybe they'll be little replicas of us, maybe they'll be little replicas of someone else. Probably there'll be a mix of both. And I expect you'll invite a few surrogate grandparents, as well. The more, the merrier, I think."

"And that's exactly why I love you."

He kissed her gently, then deepened the embrace without

thinking about it, free to love her without worrying about ruining his plan. His stupid, wonderful, misguided plan to find a wife. After a minute he backed her toward the sofa. They tumbled onto it. Clothing flew every which way as they laughed and teased and struggled not to fall off the couch.

He watched her face as he sank into her, watched the love she didn't hide, watched the pleasure come to her.

"I do believe, darlin', that this is the best-laid plan I've ever had."

She started to laugh at the double entendre, then he kissed her, stealing the laughter and replacing it with love...and tenderness...and a promise of everything wonderful in life.

* * * * *

Be sure to look for Chase's story, coming soon from Susan Crosby...and Silhouette Desire!

THE BABY OF THE MONTH CLUB

RITA Award Winning Author

MARIE FERRARELLA's

miniseries continues with her brand-new Silhouette single title

In The Family Way

Dr. Rafe Saldana was Bedford's most popular pediatrician. And though the handsome doctor had a whole lot of love for his tiny patients, his heart wasn't open for business with women. At least, not until single mother Dana Morrow walked into his life. But Dana was about to become the newest member of the Baby of the Month Club. Was the dashing doctor ready to play daddy to her baby-to-be?

Available June 1998.

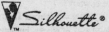

Silhouette®

Find this new title by Marie Ferrarella at your favorite retail outlet.

Look us up on-line at: http://www.romance.net PSMFIFWAY

COMING NEXT MONTH

#1135 THE SEDUCTION OF FIONA TALLCHIEF—Cait London
The Tallchiefs

Fiona Tallchief was all rebel and raw energy, but she had finally come home to Amen Flats, Wyoming, to settle down. And according to a Tallchief family legend, April's *Man of the Month*, sexy Joel Palladin, was destined to be Fiona's husband. But when Fiona discovered the secret of Joel's parentage, he knew he'd have to carefully seduce this "battlemaiden"... into marriage.

#1136 THE VIRGIN AND THE VAGABOND—Elizabeth Bevarly
Blame It on Bob

Virginal and *still single,* Kirby Connaught launched Operation Mankiller to destroy her nice-girl rep, and perennial playboy James Nash was eager to be her coach. But when local bachelors finally came calling, would James ruin his *own* reputation by committing to only Kirby, forever?

#1137 TAKEN BY A TEXAN—Lass Small
The Keepers of Texas

Socialite Lu Parsons didn't aim to become the best-little-tease-in-Texas when she asked taut-bodied Rip Morris to take care of her, uh, virginity problem. But circumstance kept them at arm's length, simmering and simpering, until Lu risked losing her heart...along with her innocence....

#1138 MATERNITY BRIDE—Maureen Child

One night Denise Torrance dropped all defenses and gave herself over to masterful lover Mike Ryan. And then her unexpected pregnancy set the couple into full swing on the "should-we-shouldn't-we" marriage pendulum. Could baby-on-the-way make these reluctants trust in the longevity of love?

#1139 THE COWBOY AND THE CALENDAR GIRL—Nancy Martin
Opposites Attract

Hank Fowler was no cowboy, but he posed anyway for a hot-hunks-of-the-West calendar contest. When pretty Carly Cortazzo found out her cover guy didn't know a lariat from a love knot would she still be roped into spending forever with a make-believe cowboy?

#1140 TAMING THE TYCOON—Kathryn Taylor

Ultratycoon Ian Bradford held tons of stocks, but lately he'd been focused on *bonds*—the late-night one-on-one kind with voluptuous Shannon Moore. But would their knock-your-socks-off sparks have Ian knocking down hopeful Shannon's door...with a marriage proposal?

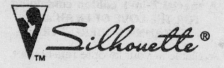